MW01043247

ELEMENTS

ROBERT GLÜCK

ELEMENTS

ROBERT GLÜCK

Ithuriel's Spear

San Francisco

A NOTE FROM THE AUTHOR

Elements was written during the heyday of my workshops at Small Press Traffic in San Francisco. Now workshop members and others are funding this edition—thank you for this Valentine!

And thanks to Ithuriel's Spear—that is, to Jim Mitchell and Francesca Rosa. Thanks also to Chris Komater and Ramsey McGlazer for their help, and to Rob Halpern as well, for joining me in my walk down Memory Lane.

Note: We dropped *of a Coffee Service* from the original title of *Elements:* I got tired of saying it and no one else seemed to remember it.

—— Robert Glück
February 14, 2013

This book was originally published in 1982 in San Francisco by Four Seasons Foundation under the title *Elements of a Coffee Service.*

Cover and book design by Plainfeather Printworks.

Cover art by Joe Brainard, used by permission of The Estate of Joe Brainard and courtesy of James S. Jaffe Rare Books and the Tibor de Nagy Gallery, New York.

ISBN 978-0-9835791-4-4
Library of Congress Control Number: 2013939901

Ithuriel's Spear is a fiscally sponsored project of Intersection for the Arts, San Francisco.

www.ithuriel.com

CONTENTS

BOB'S ELEMENTS

by Eileen Miles

ON THE OCCASION of this wonderful fresh printing after thirty years of Bob Glück's *Elements* (1983), I'd like to go public with a few things I've always thought about him. He is that thing you hear about once in a while, a writer's writer. It usually means that this person has affected a lot of readers, specifically readers who write, and it has changed the way they write. In the world of writers there is such a thing as the field, we are also always calling it the community, or even a "school." It's a something that gets turned out in your career, an ideal real space apart from selling our books and explaining them to get grants. In this field writing zips, darts and pauses like a very beloved but wild animal, and Bob is a master of knowing and watching that creature. Bob is way ahead of so many of us, who quietly and loudly thank him and even more quietly go: I'll take that.

He has many imitators. We are Bob's pods. He's kind of a one-man avant garde and a generous one for writing for years a rich lineup of smart and influential books. When we think experimental, do we think warm? That's the surprise. Bob's work is warm, hot. His work is sexy and often very beautifully graphic. He's taught gaggles of people how to write about sex, much to the consternation sometimes of his ex-lovers, and also his writing occurs in a net, under the tent of new narrative which may or may not include Kathy Acker, Dennis Cooper, Kevin Killian, Dodie Bellamy, Bruce Boone, Sam D'Allesandro, Camille Roy but mostly Bay Area authors, all West Coast. This is a school of fiction writers friendly to poetry and theory. Here on the West Coast we've got room.

Bob's books, before I get lost in the foam of my enthusiasm, Bob's fiction is actually quite friendly yet he cuts with a knife. Bob's gift to the history of letters I think is the uncanniness of his flow. He pulls down the page like a shade, it's masterful what he does. His page is more filled with light than words, really. More filled with temperature too. Why Bob's work is so unique and important is chiefly that he has taken vanguard styles and his influences are many and translated them (like Roland Barthes does) into something verging on cozy. This sounds absurd, but it's true. He takes the chill out of postmodernism and lets the warm human body think about itself. There's a melancholy in it that often animates the best poetry. That's what you get for example in his "story" "Safety" when its narrator breaks out of sleep into his house looking for a ring. A magical search. Only to step on a dog bone! Some would argue that the best poetry is prose, and Bob is about the only illustration for that theory that could possibly ever stick. Feeling is almost material in his hands. And his hands become atmosphere and the atmosphere becomes about the particularity of time and place. Which butts up gracefully against the infinite:

"Everyone was reading Jung and basking in a noble light which elevated our problems into pleasant abstractions."

Bob is a master of the shock of presence. His narrator is typically wise and befuddled. And in awe of the troubling implications of love and desire. These familiar and sexy stories, his very first collection, read to me like fables. His narrator wants me to know, even when he doesn't. Which is why this old collection is bright and new, not feeling the weight of time at all. Each body dissolves in its own consequence or dilemma. And what do we do? We just learn to watch. We just learn to stay here. Thanks, Bob.

SANCHEZ AND DAY

ONE MORNING I was walking Lily around 29th and Sanchez. Lily, whose motto is better safe than sorry, trotted not too far ahead, avoiding Dobermans and saying hello to pedestrians, gravely accepting their compliments—her gold eyelashes and extravagant tail. A Chevy pickup turned the comer in front of me and I probably looked too hard at the man in the passenger seat, who had a profile. All at once they started yelling "faggot" and "fucking faggot." I had been in a happy mood and with the last of my ebullience I gave them the finger, which I instantly regretted because the truck screeched to a stop and lurched into a three-point turn. There were four, they were laughing and yelling. Lily and I took off. We ran down Sanchez and turned back down the corner of Day along with the truck. One of them missed me with a beer can. They were laughing and driving parallel to us, but then we cut across Day, leapt up a retaining wall and through a cyclone fence by way of a hole I knew about. The fence surrounded a large field where I sometimes walk Lily late at night, giving her an opportunity to roam around a little on her own and enjoy some damp plant and earth smells.

If they didn't separate the advantage was mine since the field had entrances on both sides. I stood in the center on cut grass in San Francisco's expensive daylight; two blocks away bells began swinging toward noon, and they wouldn't attack someone in broad daylight unless of course they would. You'll understand my fear because television has trained us to understand the fear of a running man. I hoped for no police cars; attacking a homosexual is not such a clear-cut offense as, say, stealing a package of processed cheese. The odor of cut grass reminded me of my mother's childhood in Denver because she always says it reminds her of that. She lived there during the summers with my great-aunt Charlotte, a regal woman who fed the children tubs of strawberries in heavy cream and bakery bread with huge slabs of butter. That was before the days of cholesterol. But Charlotte advocated health food, brown rice and no sugar, which took some independence fifty years ago. She had plenty to spare. I remember after Uncle Harry's funeral the doorbell rang and an immense basket of fruit from Denver was delivered into my mother's hands. The delivery man said very soberly, "Mrs. Isaacs wanted to be especially sure you received this message from her. Wash it before you eat it." Then I recalled my mother's recent phone conversation with Charlotte, who said, "You were such a pretty girl, are you still pretty?" And my mother replied, "Charlotte, I'm pushing sixty." My mother, who is first and foremost a granddaughter, a daughter, sister, cousin, niece, wife, mother, sister-in-law, aunt and grandmother. So far the incident was nothing much and it had happened fast but with the sluggishness that precedes violence, so I tried to reassure myself with the safety of family memories of childhoods and old ages.

On the other hand, I had ample time to remember Kevin's bashed-in teeth and Bruce getting rousted and then rousted again by the police, and the Halloween when a man yelling "queer" charged Ed and me with a metal pipe; and to recall an acquaintance, hardly a face even, who one day sat on the blue chenille of the couch in my kitchen. He was murdered by someone he brought home, the neighbors saw the killer's face on and off during the night. That's the logical conclusion to this catalog of betrayals: the murderer takes you when you're naked and expect tenderness and each by agreement is host to the other's vulnerability. The sky clouded over allowing the green, which had been overexposed, to relax into its full color. Recalling these events did not necessarily indicate great extremity, they are not isolated in the way the grammar of sentence and paragraph isolate them. The threat of physical violence makes one part of the whole. College and my literary education agreed that I should see myself as a random conjunction of life's possibilities, certainly an enviable, luxurious point of view. But it's hard to draw on that as a model when four men are chasing you down the street. What life will that model sustain, and when aren't we being chased? The truck circled, pulled over at the entrance on 30th, the men piled out. I waited until they were out of the truck, then exited from the opposite side with Lily keeping close to my legs. Her eyes were dilated; she was vibrant and totally thrilled by the escape. We ran down to Church, turned the corner and slipped into a produce market.

The store was filled with strawberries and the odor of strawberries. I picked two baskets, making sure they were red on the bottom as well as on top, that they weren't moldy, that they smelled strong and healthy. People from Thailand ran the store and oddly, it seemed to me, they had the country-western music station playing. "Stand by Your Man" by Tammy Wynette, Willie Nelson's intimate version of "Georgia on My Mind," intelligent song—and the Eagles' song that begins by drawing out the beautiful word *desperado*. Then there was the kind of song I like a lot, where two people exchange verses answering and explaining. He worked on the dayshift and her husband worked on the nightshift. They lived in Pittsburgh and you could call them the Pittsburgh Steelers because, in voices resonant with country-western pain that made the joke dimensional, they stole love and pleasure whenever they got the chance. You might think that I like the song because I identify but that would be wrong. Their love was a child's secret hiding place for chocolate, hidden in the difference between their needs and their lives. It's true that I carry in my spine, wrists and knees the glance of a man I passed three years ago walking up 18th Street, and the shock I felt on seeing that he was completely to my taste. But the difference between these plaintive singers and myself is greater. The difference: walking on 29th a bunch of men in a truck yelled "faggot" at me.

The song ended and then I heard the sound of brakes screeching and then one, two, three, thud!—somebody's in trouble. We looked through the window to see the pickup piled into a telephone pole. A fender was balled up like tinfoil and they stood there wearing uncertain smiles, looking small and bewildered. I picked out the attractive one and when he turned I saw he was holding his hands in front of a mess of blood on his face. I stood a minute, enjoying the sheer pleasure of breathing in and out. I resolved to make my bed, throw away papers, read Gramsci's *Prison Notebooks,* have an active, no, a famous social life.

Of course that makes for a satisfying if frivolous ending. What really happened was that the men and the truck disappeared except from my imagination. I had angry dreams. Even in my erotic fantasies I couldn't banish a violence that twisted the plot away from pleasure to confusion and fear. And what I resolved was this: that I would gear my writing to tell you about incidents like the one at Sanchez and Day, to put them to you as real questions that need answers, and that these questions, along with my understanding and my practice, would grow more energetic and precise.

WHEN BRUCE WAS 36
(GOSSIP AND SCANDAL)

WHEN BRUCE WAS 36 he learned the name and address of his real mother and introduced himself to her. At first I thought that was all, but to my surprise Bruce and Jane saw a lot of each other. I was surprised because of what I took to be his waning confidence in the efficacy of mother love, both his mother's for him and his for the world. When I asked Bruce what he and his mother had in common he replied, "She's my mother." It was an answer that had more questions than the question. I took it to mean that since Jane didn't raise him, in their relationship the biological fact stands uppermost. "Anything else?" "No, in fact I think we irritate each other."

I purposely forgot to ask Bruce about his new relationship; it was too big and knotty to broach, the characters wandering through their bodies and their congested structures of need and option. Usually when Bruce and I are together we seem to be on the edge of our lives looking in, prodding and enticing from realization to realization. This is true even, or especially, of gossip, to measure our common assumptions. As Rabbi ben Ezra said, "Why bother to tell a story if you aren't going to include the meaning of your life?" To subsidize the story?—I add with a question mark. Yet a bond between a narration and a life generates a rightness surrounded by surprise and applause unmatched for its high horses. Each detail that I learned about Bruce's reunion filled me with sleep, a sign for me that emotion is at hand, and I had two dreams about it.

In the first a woman rushes through woods on a fresh, moony night with her baby wrapped in bunting against a light breeze. A resonant voice from above, a phrase murmured, repeated by the mother: *flesh of my flesh, flesh of my flesh, flesh of my flesh.* Something is wrong though; she opens the blanket, looks up at us and shouts, "This isn't the flesh of my flesh. It's a giant pine cone. This is completely inaccurate!"

I wanted to approach these issues with laughter while I dreamed them into metaphor, a satisfying if temporary solution. I wrote the dream in my journal, another temporary solution: documentation with the understanding that the world in the form of myself will discover and appreciate these fragments tossed up by myself dressed as a ruined civilization. This particular dream seems very loud to me, it shouts the way some nursery rhymes do. Wasn't he "of her flesh" and didn't he become a block of wood as far as she was concerned? From century to century things grow more estranged, said Walter Benjamin on hashish in Marseilles. He's wandering around a murky harbor like *Port of Shadows* and naturally the names of the ships convey great meaning, fraught as they are with departure. Against that fact of life, that estrangement, I want to balance Jane's irritation. She seems intact and upright. In Bruce there's an element of fatality but some inspection shows it follows rather than commands. Didn't Bruce have the mobility to assess and to act? I'm asking this question about myself; one voice elbows the others aside and says, "Given the options! Society as a whole—"and then I have to add white, male, middle class and from the total subtract homosexual, but the question still stands.

Like yourself, Bruce didn't ask to be born, and certainly not to enough mothers and fathers to constitute an evening of bridge. Bruce once showed me a photo of his adopted parents which surprised me, they looked so fit and well-groomed. His mother wore a yellow pants suit. They smiled brightly, anonymous. For me the photo's light source was Bruce's adoption. It's the question of identity and double identity, given two sets of projections, that lies behind my second dream in which Bruce discovers he has an identical twin—delight—whose name is Bruce and has Bruce's glasses and reading habits—puzzlement— and whose lover is named Jonathan and who wrote a book called *My Walk with Bob* and has the same fingerprints— mounting anxiety as Bruce sees his life usurped little by little. Bruce 2 asks Bruce, "Am I twice or half as much?" In the background we hear a plague of cicadas emerging for their seventeen-year visit.

What if Jane said, "If I had it to do over again I would not have had a child." I was very relieved to hear my father say that once and felt close to him in my anger. A photo of our auras would have shown anger sheeting off our skin. I countered with, "If I had to do it over again I might not have had parents." Would I be equal to a real answer? Would you? Or would we form the question and discussion into an olive pit to suck on thoughtfully but not crack open.

Isn't that the mental point of departure for someone ringing the doorbell of a mother who put him up for adoption? What could this mean to someone living in the world, a world that is continuous and against us, starting with the wall beside our bed, going out through the city and our lives—how do you account for facts from the outside? Facts from disparate lives? What does the passage of time mean to each of us? I reshape a third grade riddle:

Why does a clock hide its face with its hands?
Shy. Ashamed. Horrified. It depends.

To enter Bruce's interior you would have to dismantle your own. More than that, "the subjectivity of another does not simply constitute a different interior attitude to the same exterior facts." Except in Henry James, where the sharing of exterior facts is the primary luxury because it allows for all the complementary interior vistas, like a French garden. (Sound of measured footsteps on gravel.)

Let's propose a new set of facts, based on money as it always must be, but this time in opposition to money and its alienations. We call it politics and it already gives a new shared definition to words like courage and kindness. For this proposition to work we must believe in the world. To believe in the world marks you oddly as a visionary. In order to change the world you must believe in it, the things that make it up, the ideas that inform these things, the connections between them. To paraphrase Benjamin, from century to century things grow less believable. We are left with a few small objects by default and must rely on placement to suggest meaning.

A person who believes in the future knocks at a door. Knock at the Gate/Beethoven's 5th/*Macbeth*/DeQuincey: "In order that a new world may step in...."

A projection:

I'm at the doorstep, feeling drowsy. An excess of meaning has attacked me, drawing a circle around every movement: I am in my heartbeat and also listening to it: stasis. Then the conventional sends its reinforcements, they charge in like a movie cavalry, they're that abstract and violent. I'm up on a knoll watching from a distance since distance is the geographics of panic and hysteria. The urge to trivialize finishes me off and these historic victories and defeats become little spider chances.

A situation where real ascendancies are not acknowledged: From Jane's point of view there must be a lack of gentility in being a writer, something slightly suspect, like going on the stage. Not adding up to having a tax man, a den. No growly cigars, no scuba diving in the Caribbean, no forgetting about history by assuming it's ourself—it's a list we've drawn up many times one way or another. I would feel a chemical heaviness, the desire to be a pine cone. Dreams, movie images of mothers who are dreams. Wicked Bette Davis of *Little Foxes,* her tyrannosaurus rex arms; or it's the Bette Davis of *Now, Voyager,* she's nurturing Paul Henreid's child—her nobility expressed in the upsweep of her hairdo, like a prow. In this region all roads lead to complicated Joan Crawford, Mildred Pierce in her modest deco kitchen, giving and giving and giving—flesh of my flesh. Then the door opens and forms of politeness mask whatever might be going on and navigate us safely past the dangerous, the imaginary and the real.

I wonder if they love each other—more, I wonder what love means in this context, in any context. What if a person falls through the void, that person might naturally want to grab hold of something. You could call that, and its million grades of refinement, love. OK, but the forms love takes can be exact opposites. I'm thinking of the utopian sixties when love was current events—and of acid. Ed always resolved the world into crystals, reflecting and refracting. The light was the first light, the light that plant cells turn toward making half of an equation; on the other side of the equal sign was life pure and simple, "as it never is." The crystal shapes brimmed with significance as crystal shapes do. The shapes were love, and a new equation set an equal sign between meaning and safety. Ed watched them; he sat quietly in the air as a circle on a white ground.

On the other hand, I saw the world in sexual motion, fucking motion, from the whole universe fucking itself on a 4-way tab of Purple Owsley, down to the threads of my clothes, the fibers in the carpet, rubbing against each other erotically. Those were the days. Everyone was reading Jung and basking in a noble light which elevated our problems into pleasant abstractions. The universe looked like a baby bottle nipple with a rubber washer connected to it, so it could fuck itself. Since the image appeared to be resolved into male and female, I asked where I was located and it replied, "You're on the band connecting the two, an intermediate place but just as aroused." Anyway, the universe was fucking and spasming and as opposed to Ed, I wanted to join in.

Certainly if you were falling through a void you would want to catch hold of something, and from a certain point of view (mine) what had more meaning than another person?

And what is a better grabbing hold of than sex? And if Ed's essential attitude was contemplative, that was hardly the way he usually acted. Usually he was a sexual center with many spokes pointed toward him. If Ed was a hub, and that expressed his quality, then around that center I planned to be the wheel. Generously construed you could say my error was tactical; he fucked before and after and I suppose if the structure of time had given him simultaneity as an option he would have used it. He was highly conscious of genitals—his own and others'—and would say, "I like the way he wears his cock," as though it were a hair style. Ed was my other and I stood riveted before his extravagances with completely silent admiration—the emphasis here is on silent. I remember walking home one evening with Lily, who sauntered a few yards ahead of me, wagging her tail in the endearing if mechanical hope that life would remain friendly to her, that affection and cans of Kal Kan and safety and car rides to the ocean would go on forever. I was looking at Lily and mulling over an incident from the Older Writers workshop that I teach. I had brought some of my work to read and Margaret rustled papers throughout, writing fast, she said, to get her thoughts down. One of the stories I read is in *Elements*, the one about getting queer-baited at Sanchez and Day. The conclusion Margaret reached was that I ought to put all the poems and stories together as one chapter, smooth them out and send them to a dog grooming magazine. I felt profoundly disoriented and started laughing; I could imagine if things were different that I might continue laughing and laughing.

I returned from this reverie standing in front of my house. I looked up at the second story window, the window to Ed's studio, and there's Ed. A trap door thuds open in my groin. He's almost naked, just blue cotton bikini briefs, and he's playing with his cock, masturbating himself. He doesn't see me. He looks fantastic. Distanced by the window and the cold street light he's a bouquet of flesh and blood, of pleasure. I see it's for the benefit of our across-the-street neighbor, a gay doctor I later found out, who slowly mounts his front steps and then appears at his Victorian window, just watching. In this way they touch each other. I never spoke to Ed about this—I could never figure out the right tack. After all, it's his life. More than that, his electric current of sex and danger that realigned itself according to every situation—that and his visual patience to enjoy six oranges on a table—were very much to my taste. But this is a positive with a negative, because this is the kind of silence in which differences become obstacles and people are lost to each other.

When I asked my friend Denise about her characteristic acid experience she said it was talk, intense talk, in order to build a bridge between herself and the Other—self and the world—meaning and safety—certainly an act of faith greater than Ed's crystals or my baby bottle nipple. I know from experience that sheer talk puts you in increasing proximity, that it has an erotic charge; personally I can think of many happy penetrations via the ear. But Denise told me that the words turned into a Niagara Falls of language, carrying the meaning downstream and over. Do you hear, "I too have been in Arcadia," just as the falls tears up the unity of the rest? No toehold in the void there. That reminds me of another friend's acid experience which had, he said, everything romance could want. They listened to Mahler while fondling each other's ears.

Well, you could press the other to your crotch or you could press him to your breast or your lips or you could just grab or build a highway of language or move your arms like semaphores in the hope that someone takes you for a landing strip or just be the hand of a deaf person singing, depending on who you are. In any case, we lovers began to see differences without cruelty. The cruelty of laughter, the cruelty of silence in the name of good taste. My mother often wished out loud that she were blind to her children's faults, as her mother was. I took this to mean she acknowledged our differences in the language available, so the perspective was critical; still, I knew she was bragging. Who wants to be colonized into sameness? I almost prefer Anita Bryant's small-town estimate of the difference between us to the liberals' or left's opinion expressed by a silence which I am supposed to appreciate, and which by denying differences denies me myself.

Let's go back to toehold. Because the more ways you touch the world, the more you are in it. I imagine Bruce visiting Jane. What is Bruce *doing* in her life? The bell doesn't answer so he walks up the driveway to the backyard—she's working in her garden. She's beautiful but what you would notice first is intelligent. Vaguely Unitarian, she gives everyone, even God, plenty of elbowroom. "I think there must be a divine presence in the universe," she says on her knees, tearing off the corner of a seed packet with her teeth and poking holes in the dirt with her thumb of sixty years. What is Bruce doing there? A record of passion, emotion? It would be unfair to speculate; psychological bulls-eyes are not the point. Like yourself, Bruce and Jane are complicated as the world. Sex makes strange bedfellows and we know from other stories that the father was not her equal. What I mainly gather, and what feels very restful too, is that at whatever juncture she did what she wanted. She gave Bruce away, got a law degree at a time women didn't, and lived comfortably alone as sort of country gentry all these years. She's up in Auburn, isolated, aging and delicate. She's in Auburn, enjoying good health, security and the affection of many friends. It finally cools off and a hot summer night sends a breeze through the screen door. "Whew," says someone, someone looking up from a game of bridge, "it's finally cooling off." Electrical storm, charged laughter, in winter storm windows and a fireplace. She always had an idea of her own good.

Bruce and Jane are not able to disguise themselves—to prearrange the nose, mouth, brow, eyes, spine and fingers. This sometimes intrudes on the ceremonious sending of coffee and sweets past taste buds while chatting agreeably. Coffee and cake. It's a perfect domestic tableau; the only thing that would make it more perfect is if they were both inanimate objects. They talk about plants. After all, he's a poet so he ought to know the language of flowers. She politely offers him an opportunity to express himself and he does. He compliments her nasturtiums, "nasties" he calls them in deference to a great aunt's usage, and her pansies, "their little Victorian faces always saying, 'no fair, no fair,' but not being able to do anything about it." He's pleased with himself—would you deny him?—showing off his years of mental ballet exercises in one gesture. Now this flight of fancy does seem a trifle eccentric to her, a little showy. It falls on slightly worried ears.

The china is plain, or else decorated with banal decals of milkmaids and shepherds so not in keeping with her personality that they express her contempt for domestic flourishes. Perhaps some Venetian blinds slice up the light as though the light were a Spanish wind cake. I'll have them eating a Spanish wind cake because I want Jane to exhale a few *Spanische Windtorte* crumbs when Bruce asks, "Are you a lesbian?" All stiff meringue, whipped cream and strawberries, like a taffeta dress or like Elizabeth's starched ruff, ruby studded. A courtier's high diplomatic exchange between the libido and civilization. One Viennese authority writes, "Could anything be so stunning, so airy, so magnificently aristocratic?" Bruce looks worried, he's eating his second piece quickly. He says, "It's very sweet," almost reproachfully, and asks, "How many calories do you think are in each section?" Jane is irritated—how should she know and besides he's obviously heading toward his third. Yet her affection for him is larger in this small failing than in his virtues. They resemble hers but she appreciates them from a distance, because their careers express variants on the most rewarding use of a life. Who would be an out-front gay and a Marxist if he did not have an idea of what actually benefits himself? People don't become political out of altruism, that's a shabby reason. We become political after ascertaining what world is in our best interest.

They are sitting and chatting and Bruce asks and Jane says no to his lesbian question without any fuss. Perhaps she was angry. But I speculate that she arranged via her relationship with Bruce for this question to be in her life, that it represents another tangent point with the world. Actually her no was said with characteristic straightforwardness and my Viennese pastry melodrama was just that, mine.

For some time I've worked with a group of women writers in their fifties and sixties, and trying to shock Bruce's mother reminds me of an incident with Mildred. Mildred is a dark elegant Jewish woman who claims any gathering with her drama and zest and allergy to tobacco. At a reading these women gave, I introduced Mildred to Carol, a young woman from my other writing group. On the phone I suggested to Mildred that she accompany Carol to some open readings, adding that Carol earned her living as a prostitute, thinking defensive and unformulated thoughts such as "Carol has a right... The oppression of women... Sex must be..." Feminism abused, because really I just wanted to scandalize Mildred who had been raised in a kosher home, like mine, and in fact like Carol's. Mildred let a polite silence go by in deference—I think—to my expectations. She smoothed her elegant voice and said, "Well aren't people the most interesting of all?"— referring to Carol or me. Either way, that put me lyrically in my place and I cherished her for it; if I was shocked by her lack of shock then the joke was on me where it belonged. So this can be a two-way street because what if the victim is larger than you? Then scandal and gossip fall back where they originated and define the boundary of the teller rather than the listener as intended.

It's scandal's defining of boundaries that interests me, what is inside and what is outside—it's one way a community organizes itself, tells itself its story about what is forbidden and expected. Bruce's mother's possible shock may have been based on a community tenet that homosexuality does not exist verbally. For example, I know a gay man who was raised—maybe not as a grand bourgeois, but many economic notches above me. His sense of himself is based on that class background; there are certain inbuilt sympathies, certain antagonisms. A person could not terrorize this man with theory, he only grows more respectful, but he is susceptible to vulgarity. So when he says he's going to the ballet or some other elevated cultural event and would you like to join him, you reply that another time you would be delighted but now you are on your way to the baths "to get your rocks off" — cruelly enjoying his expressions of dismay alternating with a polite interest that grows increasingly transparent, and you blandly continue with, "It's been a full week and I'm really horny." What a betrayal! And what if you willed into the decaying conversation such formulas as "well hung," and "seafood" for sailors, and other idioms from the no-nonsense dictionary of pleasure: top man, versatile action, Greek passive, French active, nipple master, cut/uncut, golden showers, French service, scat, toys—they are more beautiful to me than the names of ships. I challenged my friend's modesty because it silenced an important aspect of his life—our life.

Writing this, I think back to "seeing differences without cruelty." After all, my friend is not the enemy. Could differences be acknowledged by means other than surprise attack? You may not think this concerns you but scandal is one way we gauge the language that flows backward and beneath our language like an ocean of silence; silence is a language too, it's the flip side of what we are permitted to say.

What we are permitted to do. There's a Cinderella story I told Bruce—I had it from Susie, a friend from high school who was once married to a cousin on my mother's side. Susie's childhood friend, Libby, had been adopted. At eighteen Libby looked up her real parents; they were rich and they invited her back. "Why don't you live with us?" Libby had been a model toehold for her parents, a fine student, a believer in self-improvement, a conscientious member of her nuclear unit. What ingratitude, I said happily. Who has more grist for blackmail, more claims on your one and only existence than your real parents?—your adoptive parents!—since they combine the urge to possess with a charitable impulse. Hearing about the American hostages in Iran for the 213th day, one of my third grade students wrote, "Whenever anyone speaks to children about hostages, we should answer, 'Children are hostages too!'" Libby shrugged off her life's commitments in one resounding gesture and left for Europe with the rich parents for an indefinite stay. It was the Riviera and if the sand was white and the sea was blue her adopted family didn't know it because she never even sent a postcard!

And now for a temporary solution:

There's a Greek myth about scandal. I forget her name, but pleasure rains across her body defining it in rivulets of Greek cloth. She races through moony woods—past a retaining wall covered by ivy, like Bruce's mother in my dream: a woman's movement through the forest, seen from above by moonlight dappling the gloomy trees of the Northwest. That she is oppressed, even by this myth, is undeniable. Also, she did what she wanted. On behalf of all the trees, now Greek and animate, I'd like to caution her, "Don't say it to anyone." I'd like them all, and the birds and the ground squirrels and spiders too, to tell her, "Don't say it to anyone—but me!" The scandal of a bastard child, an illicit lover. She tells the reeds. She says, "My life and the world are one. Forget-me-not." When they repeat her story she becomes a windflower for faithlessness, or a chrysalis for changeability, or a willow for contrition, or a fern for tenderness, or a mirror for themes, or an x for sexuality, or a pillar for certainty, or the sun for meaning, or a strawberry for the heart, or a fortress for safety, or a telephone for gossip, or a torrent for great feeling, or a planet or a ship or a mesa or a star or a continent or an element or a season.

SAFETY

I WOULD START AWAKE at three in the morning and search passionately for an hour, stirring drawers and then returning to the same drawers and stirring again. It was an oval of clear quartz that had two names, Venus Hairstone and Cupid's Arrows, set on a rectangle of silver. I could see through the stone to the silver lake bottom. A few gold lines—vectors—shot through the stone moving into it, arrows or hair. Like a melancholic I made the loss allegorical, relating it to nostalgia for language that's unaware of its approaching death: "Cupid and my Campaspe played at cards for kisses; Cupid paid." I moved through the four rooms trying to shake off the terrible presence of space which the lost ring insisted on. Still, I am always *perversely* looking for loss and calling it sensibility.

One night my eyes opened at three and I got up and out of bed. After the pain that made me wave my arms and hold my breath and hit the top of my head again and again so as not to cry out and wake up Ed—after it subsided and the subsequent nausea subsided, I went back to see what I had stepped on that broke the skin of my arch. It was a bone.

It belonged to my dog. No use being mad at *her.* You could never expect "Don't leave your bones—" to catch hold in a dog.

Still, that seemed to put the right parenthesis on my ring-searching period. I hobbled to the kitchen and sat trembling. This is certainly the safest room and also the most false, I thought, because everything refers to the past, quoting and quoting. The copper pots mean Country French, the white curtains are Victorian shifts of muslin, the pine table means the Old West, the head of cabbage means the Great Depression, the framed Holstein is a borrowed agrarian childhood and so on.

This is a backward kind of poem written in the evening of a chilly fall day. The cups hang in a row over the sink like quotation marks around the word "safety."

SEX STORY

BRIAN UNDID THE BUTTONS of my levis one by one, pulled down my pants and Egyptian red cotton briefs; white skin and then my cock springs back from the elastic—"hello, old timer." A disappointing moment when possibilities are resolved and attention localized, however good it's going to be. So it's going to be a blow job—that's nice. So it's going to be sex—nice, but less than the world. That blow job defined the situation, then a predictable untangling of arms and legs and stripping off shoes and clothes, my jeans, his corduroys, lighting sand candles, putting on records, closing straw blinds, turning back sheets, turning off lights. Brian has a way of being naked a few minutes at a distance—he politely averts his eyes so I can study him unselfconsciously.

"From his small tough ears, his thick neck came down to his shoulders in a long wide column of muscles and cords that attached like artwork to the widened 'V' of his clavicle, pointing the way to his broad, almost football padded shoulders and then down to those muscular arms, covered with blond hair. The tits were firm, and never jiggled, though the nipples were almost the size of a woman's, and seemed always to be in a state of excitement. A light patch of blond hair was growing like a wedge between them, and a long racing stripe of blond hair led the eye down over the contour of his rippling stomach muscles, past the hard navel, and streamlined down to a patch of only slightly darker pubic hair. There, in all its magnificence hung the 'Doug.' Its wide column of flesh arched out slightly from his body, curving out and downwards in its solidness to the pointing tip of its foreskin where the flesh parted slightly exposing the tip of a rosebud cockhead. The width of the big cock only partially hid a ripe big sack behind it, where two spheric globes of his balls swelled out on either side of it. The cock hung down freely, without the slightest sign of sexual arousal, and still it spanned downward a full third of the boy's young strong legs.

"'Turn around slowly,' Cliff said to Rags, unbuttoning his own shirt and pulling it back off his torso....'"

That was from *Fresh from the Farm* by Billy Farout, pp. 20-21. I want to write about sex: good sex without boasting, descriptive without looking like plumbing, happy, avoiding the La Brea Tar Pits of lyricism. Brian is also golden, with a body for clothes, square shoulders, then nothing but the essentials decked out with some light and pleasant musculature. He carries his shoulders a little hunched—the world might hit him on the head—which goes with a determined niceness that can become a little grim, like taking the bus to the LA airport to meet me. But if he has his blind spots, Bruce, Kathy, Denise and I said in various combinations over cups of coffee—well, who doesn't. It's that this one doesn't correspond to ours. Five years ago Brian painted a picture of a house and had many delusions about it. Finally he went to live in the relative safety of its rooms. I can understand that. Brian looks like anyone. Rags looks like no one; he's an alluring nightmare that reduces the world to rubble. Really, I could never grasp Brian's looks, a quality I admire. When I understand his face, solve it into planes and volumes, factor in blond hair and green eyes, then he turns his head a little, the essential eludes me and I must start all over. Sometimes he's intact as a fashion model exuding sunlight. Sometimes he's a fetus, big unfortunate eyes and a mouth pulled down, no language there, fingers and toes waiting to be counted.

I knelt and returned his blow job, his body tensed toward me and his cock grew in my mouth according to his heartbeat, each pulse a qualification that sent me backward to accept more. I was not completely in favor of his cock—it seemed indecisive—but he didn't care about it either. When I praised him—"the charm of its shape"—he shrugged and the compliment didn't register. It was his ass, full and generous, that we concentrated on.

He more or less pushed me onto the bed and tumbled after me, raising our exchange a level by blowing me while looking into my eyes. He's giving me pleasure and looking at me, keeping me focused. I'm acknowledging that. There's no way to dismiss this by saying I'm lost in a trance, by pretending I am not myself. Still, I make an escape clause—I say: I put myself entirely in your hands and what I know you desire is to put yourself in mine, so I demand what I know you want me to want. I stood and commanded him to blow me, to do this and that: crawl behind and rim me while I masturbate myself. Brian replied, "As James Bond used to say, 'There's no mistaking that invitation.'" A tongue in your ass is more intimate than a cock anywhere; I receive the sensation inside my groin, in my knees and nipples and wrists. Now this was like a porno movie, or the sex ads in the gay newspapers:

Top (Father, Cowboy, Coach, Cop) wants Bottom (Your prisoner and toy)—and conversely.
29-34? Small waist, W/M, Fr a/p, Delicious tongue worship your endw. Lean back & watch yr hot rod get super done, Sir. Don't any of you with long poles want to be shucked down and get some down-home Fr?
EXHIBITIONISM, j/o, facesitting,
Close Encounters in Venice.

What made it sexy? Probably the posture that isolated sex, isolated fantasy. He blew me and I took one step backward. He murmured, loving to crawl forward. The gesture, economical and elegant as a hawk's wing, pointed toward a vista that was not geographical.

I lifted him and we kissed passionately, our first real kissing filled with deep tongues and assy fragrance, running my tongue over his lips, each tooth defined by a tongue, our saliva tasted the same, he played with our cocks and I carried him to the—no, first he knelt and licked me, licked my feet and legs, tongued between my toes. "I don't like pain but I don't mind a good spanking." I obliged, spanking him on one cheek, then the other, while he blew me and masturbated himself. Then I had to piss and Brian made coffee. What if friendship and love are extras tagged onto sexuality to give it a margin of safety, of usefulness, and the relations between subject and object, usually dismissed as a set of perversions, were the heart of sex? Brian slipped into the bathroom while I was thinking and pissing. To my surprise he knelt and drank from my cock, looking at me. I wonder what I'm getting into, I said to myself, getting into it.

Still in the bathroom: "I sit on your lap and you talk to me like a father." What if desire and power take the form of "Law" as we experience it, whether as the "father" or the "cop?" "Have you been a good boy?" "I have a special treat for you." "Are you going to do a good job?" Whispered while tonguing his ear and raining kisses on his neck and cheek— all the language of blackmail and instrumentality, its context shifted to pleasure. Brian dutifully replied to his father's cock, not daring to raise his eyes. These few phrases established father and son, where desire is accumulated and forbidden, yet we remained animals exploring pleasure, teasing prostates with inserted forefingers up to the first and second knuckle, learning by heart each other's cock better than our own, needing to touch all his skin with my tongue: the tonguing of nipples until erect and then little bites accepted resistingly, tongue around the ears, inside the head, his curls of blond hair a county line for a tongue going out of town, down the backbone, pause, into the crack, pause, testing the asshole— clean as a whistle, tidy boy—tapping with the slightest pressure, knocking again and again to produce a moan, the straining backward, the gasp of a penetration. Caressing him there satisfied me as though I were touching all of Brian at once.

That got old and the kettle whistled. We settled back in bed with the coffee. There was no way around it, he loved me. It was plain to see in his melting eyes. More, in the steadiness of that melting gaze: he made me more naked than without

37

clothes. I hadn't been loved that way for years; my relief was so fierce you could call it passion. Brian loved me quickly and thoroughly, without a credit check on my personality. I felt abashed.

Responding to my thought he told me the story of his falling in love (which I fill in):

Brian and two women friends traveled from LA to San Francisco to spend Halloween with me. Brian wanted us to portray Earth, Wind, Fire and Water, and accordingly made costumes and masks which he brought along. They were brown, baby blue, scarlet and royal blue, with matching sequins and feathers. I forget which was mine but I rebelled when I saw the scanty muslin toga. "I'll make my own costume," I said, and so we went as Earth, Fire, Water, and a bumblebee. I drank—scared and belligerent. A blur of emotions. In a bar: "I'm a BUMBLEBEE, asshole." We returned home; the scenario indicated passionate happy lovemaking for hours and hours. I dreaded it. Instead I drank a half pint of brandy on top of the evening's beverages. That was October. I hadn't divested myself of the summer's construction project in LA, an escalating nightmare of fraud and anxiety. Ed and I formally separated in June; I desired him in the same way that I still require a cigarette, a physical call. I hardly drink, I never drank. Depressed, I ate Viennese pastry. Ed said he knew when I was upset because I left doilies around the kitchen.

I drank myself into a crying jag. I peeled off my sweaty cigarette-smelling bumblebee outfit and cried on Brian's hot skin for hours. Sometimes I paused, then a stronger wave would submerge me and carry me up. Crescendo. The pain registered as isolation. My body really hurt, my skin hurt, so

I decided I'd better eat bread to absorb the alcohol. Besides, crying had made me claustrophobic. It was five in the morning. I got up feeling like Monday's wash, put on one of my abject T-shirts and sat down in the kitchen, wearily sniveling and cramming saltines down my throat. "And that," said Brian, "is when I fell in love with you."

We were on our sides more or less tangled up. His free hand meditated on the slimness of my waist, the power of my shoulders and chest. I basked in his general radiance. I loved his waist and the gold of his skin, I wanted to fold myself into it. Then he slid down and kissed my cock the way you kiss lips. He said, "I love your cock." He said it with more fervor than customarily applied to a sweet nothing, and so lapidary that I assured myself I would remember it during that amount of "forever" which is to be my portion. I've been reading Jane Austen. He said it to my cock's face, and I thought Oedipally, "A face a mother could love." "How's your mother?" And, "How's her emerald collection?" I liked to hear him recite her stones. I think Brian felt he betrayed her a little, that my eagerness and the question itself was not in the best taste; "Gimme a break," he would say. And here I am justifying his fears. But really I viewed her collection as a victory, a personal domain wrested from so much that was not hers. I liked its lack of utility and sexual shimmer. I liked the war that each piece represented, complete with siege, ground strategy and storming the fort. Her collection was an Aladdin's hoard, not an investment. She had: (1) A diamond and emerald bracelet, groups of four each alternating around. (2) A diamond ring that Brian says doubles as a Veg-a-matic. (3) A diamond and gold brooch set on an inch-wide gold bracelet (Brian's favorite). (4&5) Two pairs of diamond and emerald clips. (6) An emerald brooch, geometric design within a rectangle. (7) Many pearls. (8) A large emerald ring. Plus opals and a few token stones.

Brian's mother angles back a little of her own power in the going currency of charm and attractiveness. She's not the Enemy. I met the enemy at a gay resort on the Russian River. It felt strange to be there, surrounded by money and its attendant—available and well-groomed flesh. Until that day I spent my vacation at a small neighborhood beach where nakedness was not so much a declaration. Each morning I took Old River Road to about five yards from the Hacienda Bridge, veered right and coasted down a steep grade that carried me back to an older level of houses and crossroads beneath the bridge. Like a dream: *there is a world underneath this one and it's here now.* I parked at the end of Hummingbird Lane, stepped over a barbwire fence and its PRIVATE sign, took a darkly congested path—maple trees and blackberry bushes—which became sunnier—manzanita and buck brush—opening out to the hot sun and an arid span of rock and sand bleached white right up to the river's channeled coolness. Naked people lay as far from each other as possible. The air was white and deadlocked from reflected heat, it made the sunbathers look like quick sketches. When I wet my lips I almost tasted the remote breeze that stirred the tops of the laurel and Douglas fir growing up the opposite hillside. I couldn't hear the river; a loud buzzing sound came from the spellbound air, the inactivity, the heat, my own breath—I either submitted to it or felt anxious.

That stretch of river held a special attraction for me. A few white alders grew on a little island. Next to the island there was a small rapids with an alder overhanging it, and someone had tied a rope around a branch. A swimmer could grab hold of the rope and be carried up by the water—lithe and quick—legs, belly, everything washed and washed. Buoyed up like that, if I submerged my head a giant roaring surrounded me. It was so pleasurable I could endure it only a few minutes. I was bored, alone, diffused—there was no ground to be me pursuing my aims, no margin for the anxiety of perspective, resolution into categories. Gradually I spent more time dangling from that rope; finally I tied myself to it although I feared drowning. What a pleasurable agony each moment is as it dilapidates into the next. The water rushed, brought my body to a point, it felt good.

My friend Sterling came up from San Francisco and stayed at a gay resort, which is how I found myself lying nakedly beside a swimming pool along with fifty other men. I was comforted by the smell of chlorine and hot cement. We looked like a David Hockney that had gotten out of hand; the sun was spinning ribbons in the water and also cooking eight thousand pounds of shellacked gay flesh. Sterling introduced me to suntan oil. His friend Tom, the enemy I mentioned before, had joined us. We repositioned ourselves to the full sun. I was on my stomach, drowsy, and Sterling absentmindedly put his hand on my left asscheek, he put his hand on my ass, he put his hand on my ass and he kept it there, he kept it there—I didn't move a muscle and basked in his hand more than in the sun, pleasure spread to the back of my legs, my lower back and my nipples—not a muscle, he'd think I was uncomfortable, his hand was hotter than the sun on my other cheek—somebody said, "Bob's got an ass like a peach." Sterling, who's black, said, "Not that much color." I suggested wintermelons. "What?" said Sterling.

"*Wintermelons...*" "What did Bob say?" asked Tom. "He said, *wintermelons,*" Sterling replied.

Tom gazed abstractly down at his unformulated body, master of all he surveyed. The afternoon passed and much conversation got said and forgotten, but information about his wealth gathered like nuggets or objets d'art set side by side on a mantle. Instead of ormolu clocks and Chinese epergnes, I counted three houses—mansions—in San Antonio, a farm in upstate New York, two houses in Florida, a ranch in the Panhandle, three houses in San Francisco, and condos in New York City and Palm Springs. These were his proud investments; he'd made this million on his own, not resting on the laurels of his inherited millions from Gulf Oil. Answering me, he said, "My watch cost $8,000. Look, it's a twenty dollar gold piece with a diamond knob, set in a gold case."

Tom furnished much food for thought. It shocked me that he was so undefined. At thirty he still had his baby fat, aimless good will. He wore the most conventional plastic leather outfits. Never in his life had he voluntarily read anything more detaining than a magazine. Was *this* the Pomeranian Earl of Rochester, his overbright eyes leering subnormally under his peruke? I expected manners, Jane Austen, nice debates as to who takes precedence at dinner, fine points. How else do you know you're different from the servants?—and the people who run your farms and rent your apartments? When I returned from the toilet he joked, "Did everything come out all right?" And later he asked it *again*.

How could all that wealth be condensed in this fatuous presence? The answer: it wasn't. The wealth stayed where it was, intangible. Maybe Tom's character grew vague by way of response. Tom doesn't live on top of his servants; his property remains as abstract as the money it equals. Even the fifty Persian carpets he treasures wait in constant breathless readiness to be traded or sold. So manners might be beside the point, the tweed and horses of his seniors a tip of the hat to feudal wealth. But how can I attack Tom's life and still defend his sexuality? When Sterling, Tom and I walked back to my car we passed a bunch of "youths" whiling away the day lounging on their pickups, and despite Tom's bank account they started yelling: "Death to Faggots," "Get Outta Town," "Kill Queers," etc.

Tom became vivid for me in one passage that afternoon. Is it surprising that the medium of his transformation should be pleasure? We were cooling off in the shallow end, watching the suntan oil slick make marbled paper patterns on the pool's surface. We acknowledged a passing physique, a body that summed up what's happening these days. Tom attempted a joke about fist-fucking that included a reference to a subway entrance. I said that I could understand the erotic charge of bondage and discipline, of water sports and so on, but I could never grasp fist-fucking's sensuality. Was it homage to the fist and arm, that masculine power engaged, taken on because inside you? Tom responded with patience and expertise, accustomed to making things clear to laymen. He said that most fist-fucking is beside the point because it stops at what he called the trap. I think that's a plumbing term. He said that the colon makes a right-hand turn and then loops up all the way to the diaphragm. He drew the arch on my torso with his forefinger. If you negotiate that turn and forge ahead, your hand is a membrane away from the heart—in fact, you can actually hold your lover's beating heart. More than that, after a while your two hearts establish a rapport, beat together, and what physical intimacy could exist beyond this?

I let out a long breath. I was a little stunned. Until then, being naked, I felt naked. Facing this vista of further nakedness, I felt dressed and encumbered as a Victorian parlor.

I joined Sterling; I lay face down on an orange plastic cot and dozed. Troubling images: We're on top of a pyramid. The Aztec priest holds a stone knife in one hand and in the other he lifts the still-beating heart above its former home, the naked warrior, whose lower back balances on a phallic sacrificial stone. He's held by half-naked priests at the hands and feet, his body still spasming and arching. That from the eighth grade. There were no undressed white people in my textbook. Perhaps the compilers felt that Indians did not possess enough being to be capable of nakedness. If I were that picture everyone's cock would be hard as the stone knife.

And this from Anne Rice's *Interview with a Vampire*: "Never had I felt this, never had I experienced it, this yielding of a conscious mortal. But before I could push him away for his own sake, I saw the bluish bruise on his tender neck. He was offering it to me. He was pressing the length of his body against me now, and I felt the hard strength of his sex beneath his clothes pressing against my leg. A wretched gasp escaped my lips, but his bent close, his lips on what must have been so cold, so lifeless to him; and I sank my teeth into his skin, my body rigid, that hard sex driving against me, and I lifted him in passion off the floor. Wave after wave of his beating heart passed into me as, weightless, I rocked with him, devouring him, his ecstasy, his conscious pleasure."

The vampire's erotic charge consists of just this meeting of heartbeats, yet our hero consumes the life he is experiencing. Rice weaves homosexuality into vampire society. Does it make the dead deader or more alive? "The pleasures of the *damned*," "the *pleasures* of the damned"; in "Carmilla," once Le Fanu underscores his vampire's grief, you are free to enjoy by proxy her lesbian embrace: "She used to place her pretty arms about my neck, draw me to her, and laying her cheek to mine, murmur with her lips near my ear, 'Dearest, your little heart is wounded; think me not cruel because I obey the irresistible law of my strength and weakness; if your dear heart is wounded, my wild heart bleeds with yours. In the rapture of my enormous humiliation....'"

So death accompanies this heart stuff. And some would say, do say, that Tom's journey through the anus is a trip to the underworld. Yet this is all very far from the harmony of Tom's description, far from the particular realm of pleasure that expresses the urge to be radically naked. Tom isn't dead, neither are his partners. As Tom and his friend get dressed, culture, ideology and conflict enter simultaneously, saying we are supposed to be alone, discontinuous. We experience this as safety. We experience as transgression the penetration of our boundaries, fusion with another, and they warn us that this transgression is fearful as death. Naturally the vampire always wears a criminal half-smile. This guilt, even if slightly embraced, even if an inch stepped toward, becomes a sexual apparatus increasing the pleasure it decreased, a second ego becoming its own opposite.

I woke up on the plastic cot in the sunlight and shade, looking at a grid of sun the cot stenciled on the cement, thinking over and over *Orfeo ed Euridice, Orfeo ed Euridice*. I forgot who I was; the music and sunlight seemed more real. It was not the composer's name, or—I think—the trip through hell. Not even the "Dance of the Furies" to which I did my situps every morning. It was the following band I recalled, "The Dance of the Blessed Spirits," so limpid and noble that I would lie back exhausted and just float.

Sterling was by my side; the rest of the pool area was mostly deserted. He told me a story about his mother which reminded me of Brian's mother and her emeralds. While Brian's mother operated in that middle-class locus of power, the parents' bedroom, Sterling's mother went outside of the house, changing the terms. Sterling grew up in San Antonio where his father, a gambler also named Sterling, had married in his forties a woman twenty years younger. Along with other business ventures, Sterling Sr. ran a "buffet flat." He usually had a mistress but age brought respectability, and now he confines himself to real estate and Adele. Sterling recalls only one fight from his childhood. He can't remember why, but Sterling Sr. slapped his mother. They were in the kitchen; Adele stood in front of a stove filled with a complicated Sunday dinner. She yelled, "You want a fight, motherfucker? I'll give you a fight!"—and she systematically threw at her husband: muffins, potatoes, roast, salad, peas, collard greens, gravy and peach pie. Sterling Sr. stood uncertainly for a moment, weighing the merits of an advance. Finally he broke for the front door. Adele followed. She continued throwing the household at him, including, Sterling said with a pang, a cranberry glass lamp with lusters. Sterling Sr. jumped in his car and started to pull away but Adele got a rifle and blew out his tires. He skidded to a service station, changed tires, and spent a few days in

Dallas. This noisy exchange triggered in Sterling's mom a meditation: its theme was power. At that time Adele worked for a travel agency. Her employers, an alcoholic white couple with liberal views, absconded to Mexico with the advance receipts for a tour of the Holy Land, leaving the agency more or less to Adele. She moved it to the black section of San Antonio and became financially independent. On one of her guided tours of Los Angeles she acquired a lover; they met there for years. All this strengthened Adele's marriage. The two went past the inspirational bitterness of events to the events themselves, and now they are enjoying their sunset years, closer than ever.

"What's a buffet flat?"

It's a railroad flat, a long maroon hallway with many rooms: one room had two men doing it, another had two women doing it, and really each room had anyone with anyone, doing it. It's a sexual buffet. You paid an entrance fee to watch or act. I like the town meeting aspect of this. Also there were stars whom the audience egged on; 1910—big hats and skirts—or the twenties, a little tunic of dark spangles. Against that antique clothing nakedness becomes more naked.

What if I am a black woman who propositions one of these talented big fish. What a smile I'm capable of, I flash him one of these. I'm wearing a black beaded tunic I mentally refer to as my star-spangled night and the streets aren't paved. Want some tequila? Just a splash. What if we're naked together, clothes tossed over a chair and he only fucks me in the missionary position. What if I ask after a while if that's all.

What if he says, "Baby, I'm just warming up, just giving you a taste." I am the bottom man and this river is the top man, lithe and muscular with two handfuls of flesh. I am a bottom, the person who really controls is the bottom and sex is the top and I arrange for it to take my streaming body and clear me of names and express me and bring me to a point. This is pleasure and I'm no fool.

Brian said, "Jackie Kennedy made the pillbox hat famous. She made Halston famous, she made sleeveless dresses famous, she made Valentino famous. She made Gucci famous." "Thrilling words," I said, "I can only add that the discovery of the individual was made in early 15th-century Florence. Nothing can alter that fact. Don't you think that's interesting? I do." Brian laughed at me and said, "You're like e=mc2, always brimful of meaning." Then he asked conversationally, "Don't you think your cock is more interesting? I do." I thought it was a likely topic and finished my coffee. "Or am I putting words in your mouth?" he continued, taking my cock in his mouth and laying his head on my lap, still looking up at my face. I replied, "I reckon I'll just kick back and get me some old-fashioned, down-home French." Brian looked like a fetus. Then he sat up and said, "We boys in the back room voted you Mr. Congeniality." "What makes me a great catch?" I asked, falling into his arms so he'd have to catch me. "Looking for compliments?" "I just want to see if our lists tally." Then, seriously, "You know, I have a very beautiful couch." By way of response Brian tickled me, which escalated into wrestling. I lost because I wanted to see what he would do with an immobilized me; he held me down and started licking my torso while I mock resisted even though I was hard. "Want a frozen Reese's Peanut Butter Cup?" he asked my extravagantly arching neck. I pictured them stacked neatly in his freezer. Coffee, Kools and peanut butter cups were Brian's staff of life. I followed him into the kitchen, past his new room arrangement that I had just admired upside down through the bedroom door.

Brian lived in a bungalow in Venice, CA—a bedroom, living room and kitchen. He furnished the living room with a mattress, a box spring, a large palm, a poster-size print of a sepia photograph of women in long skirts carrying rifles in the Mexican Revolution, and another poster of a Hiroshige woodblock print (*36 Views of...*). The room was spotless and these five elements constantly found new spatial relationships. I followed him: a small deco kitchen with a total of four dishes, three cups, two one-quart stainless steel saucepans, mismatched flatware for two and a half, and a knife. I liked the cups, Mexican enamel with a decal of an innocent nosegay.

We stood in the dark kitchen kissing; that got old. He wanted to sit on my lap. I was so aroused I was wide open. We mutual masturbated like that and kissed—I was gasping. I caught our reflection in the window and it was funny to see us so localized inside these giant sensations of pleasure, my hips and muscles permanently cocked.

That got old so I carried him to the kitchen table where he squatted like a frog and I fucked him. My own body knows what his experienced: each time my cock touched a certain point hot and icy shivers radiated outward. I burn and freeze. If you have a man's body that is what you would feel. A cock's pleasure is like a fist, concentrated; anal pleasure is diffused, an open palm, and the pleasure of an anal orgasm is founded on relaxation. It's hard to understand how a man can write well if he doesn't like to be fucked. There's no evidence to support this theory; still, you can't be so straight that you don't submit to pleasure. Ezra Pound claimed his poetry was a penis aimed at the passive vulva of London. Perhaps that's why his writing is so worried, brow-furrowed. We dallied with coming for a while but decided no. Brian loved to be carried and pleasure made me powerful, sent blood to my muscles and aligned them. I lifted him from the table and fucked him in the air.

It was great sex—not because of the acrobatics, not even because he loved me and showed it and showed it, but because we were both there, very much of us, two people instead of two porno-movie fragments. Brian knelt in front of me, sucking the cock that fucked him. That's one—among many—of the things I wouldn't do. Don't do too often. It's not so bad, but all I think is now I'm doing this and what disease will I get. I quickly brush the cock with my hand like kids sharing a bottle of coke, certain that no germs are killed, just so something besides my lips touches it first. I admired Brian's range and mobility; his sexuality makes little concession to the world. I contrasted him favorably with myself. Brian is more sexually alive than anyone I know. A shower of sparks spills off his skin like inside a foundry. I'm a little more cautious, a little less generous. Let's say I had to avert my eyes.

I had to piss, Brian smiled, I laughed—a light went on about all the coffee he kept feeding me. Ed, whose dream life still seems definitive, described pissing into epic Busby Berkeley waterfall fantasies, erotic masterpieces of technical know-how. I presented to Brian the difficulty of pissing when hard, but in the spirit of the great director he assured me that when there's a will there's a way. All the same, these particular golden showers were intermittent. Kneeling, he put his head between my legs—I pissed on his back, then slowly in his mouth. Because the temperature was all the same I couldn't tell what was cock, mouth or urine, like pissing in a lake, just feeling warmth and a pressure outward. I envied Brian the clarity of his position.

Not sex, but my concern for you makes this story vulgar. You see I named it before you could. Brian and I were both so powerful, admiring each other's power. Surely power and sexuality seek each other out, even if ultimately they are held in a suspension. But our force was opposite to the kind that oppresses and controls, so it engendered permissiveness and generosity. Like the strategies of the two mothers who wanted to reclaim their lives: on the one hand, power lies in understanding the given terms and using them as leverage; on the other hand, power changes the terms. In literature, the former is *technique*—I want to create beautiful things (precious stones); the latter, *strategy*—I want a dynamic relation with my audience (my husband).

I scooped Brian up, kissed him and carried him back to bed. He asked me if I'd like to hear about his confinement in a mental institution. He asked so politely that I understood he wanted to tell me about it: "You have to understand I repeated the story about 498 times during the first two days—doctors are even more curious than you—but I'll try to make it fresh." (It's true he talked as though he were composing a letter.) He began, "Well, Bobbo, it's like this:

"I'd been whittling my life down so that smoking cigarette became an actual activity. I just broke up with a boy named Aaron who lived about three blocks away. I used to visit him in his new apartment and model for a painting called *The Junkie*. It showed me sitting in a pile of garbage with a needle in my arm."

"You sat there with a needle in your arm?"

"After I went nuts, Aaron told me he never found anyone who could hold the pose as long. I was taking a visual perception course taught by a woman named Edith Hammer. She was a great teacher; she'd show different works from different times and compare their visual components. After my second class I had an acute guilt attack, rushed to an art supply store and bought a large square canvas, paints and brushes. I rushed home to the apartment I had shared with Aaron but now occupied alone, and started painting.

"At first the idea seemed lyrical and intelligent: to make a cross section of reality in the form of a house."

"Sounds like an idea to me. Meaning and Safety."

"The windows were shaped like coffins and corresponded to gravestones above. The windows opened on a blank horizon. Above was a cemetery scene illustrating a story from my mother's childhood; it showed my grandmother and my aunt sitting under a tree, my mother as a child running to them, and my uncle as a baby watching the whole thing from behind the tree. It was done in mottled brilliant colors and I was very excited about it.

"I would wake up every morning and see something else and keep working, drawn deeper into it. I saw duality in everything; the painting helped me break down reality into its basic components and I thought if I saw past the duality I'd get to the nitty-gritty. Meanwhile it was getting a little scary. I titled the painting *The Conception and Evolution of Brainchild's Unity Theorem,* and when I printed that on a piece of paper and thumbtacked it to the lower corner, the gesture completed the delusion. I thought I had brought the symbol to reality—that some presence came from

52

my painting through the white of the clouds which were unpainted, thus being a void. Then I had the terrifying conviction that I somehow evolved myself through the painting to be God.

"The more I tried to reason it out, the deeper I got. I tried burning the frame I had made in my bathtub, thinking if I partially destroyed the painting I could save myself. I was afraid if I burned the whole painting I might die or the world might end. I started schlepping the painting. I took it to school—'nice'—and then to Miss Hammer—'spiritual.' I wanted to throw up.

"Finally after a visit to my friend Mary Dell (with the painting)—no one seemed to be able to deal with what was going on with me. I called Mary Dell back that night and she drove me to the hospital where I lied and said I had insurance and committed myself. The admitting shrink thought I was tripping."

Brian had finished. I felt trapped by his story: his years felt like a graph with sadness as both scales. It struck me that the same qualities—generosity, emotional presence—that paved the way for all this distress also made him good at love. Should I charge in and set up squatter's rights in his experience? He wasn't dejected, didn't call for support or even sympathy. Just because of that, he seemed to test my aptitude for sympathy and support. I feared Brian might want to be saved, and how could I do that? Then I realized he just wanted me to pay attention. With tremendous exertion I asked him some questions. How long was he in? Nine months. Jesus! Did they try to cure him of being gay? (I squeezed his cock.) Yes, although they didn't succeed. (He squeezed my cock.) But in the end the violence of Brian's story was so much a condensation of dream to me that I was falling asleep; sleep was a cliff that I fell off, drifting slowly as a parsley flake in a jar of oil. Did he have to wear a uniform? Yes. They sedated him most of the time.

Our bodies had turned around. We looked up at the ceiling, absentmindedly playing with our own or each other's cocks, which enhanced my detached response to Brian's story. As a postscript he added: "Aaron embraced the Bahai faith and swore himself to celibacy. He now lives in a trailer in Champagne, Minnesota, and calls me occasionally to ease the Way. The painting ended up in my shrink's office closet. I moved to Los Angeles and found a job as the manager of the toddler's department at Saks." (I see him looking like the sun in his linen suit. He's saying—with his hand over his heart— to a bullying child, "Hey, gimme a break.")

In the silence that followed we applied ourselves to each other's body more creatively; we dribbled on some Vaseline Intensive Care lotion while Brian speculated that probably gay men have younger cocks because of the oils and lubricants. Truman Capote wrote that we also have youthful necks and chins, I added, because of all the sucking. I recalled an Isherwood quotation: "Of course it would never have occurred to any of them to worry about the psychological significance of their tastes." I copied this passage on my journal page after three recipes for potato salad.

I don't think "disturbed" people are more healthy than "normal" ones, but sometimes there is a fine line, or no line at all, between disturbed and oppressed. Driven crazy is more like it. Are oppressed people more sexual? Other forms of discourse—languages of production and ownership—have been denied us or disowned. By default we are left with sex and the emotions—devalued as Cinderella at the hearth. And then we become—maybe—Cinderella at the ball. Then we are blamed for embracing sexuality and we will be a bone in the throat of people who don't. It's the same with the popular cultures of gays, people of color, the working class. They are feared because they draw energy away from "productive goals." And they are colonized, neutralized and imported into our stagnant mainstream culture. Sex is a sign of life. If sex is relegated to gays as a sign of our devalued state—becoming the shimmer of jewels—it's strange to me that the Left hasn't broached the topic of pleasure. You could say the Left leaves it to Freud, but where is pleasure in all his systems and epi-systems? In all that dominant where is the tonic, the home key?

Brian asked, "What would you like?" A thought sailed by, "It would be nice if you...." Inspiration failed—I was dejected, couldn't grasp the rest. It was growing light. I felt a little scared to be doing this for so many hours, a little "disturbed." I thought of the Marquis de Sade, the business of being perpetually feverish, energy spiraling out because it's mental, disconnected from physical rhythms, busy, busy, busy. I wanted my borders back; I wanted to curl into myself intact as a nautilus shell and let my sleeping mind group and regroup to absorb and master this experience. I said, "Masturbate me as slowly as you can." We lay on our backs, side by side and head to foot. This is really a solitary activity for two in that your attention equals your sensation, and the hand on the other's cock requires as little care as the hand that grasps a branch in the Russian River. We masturbated each other slowly, achingly gathering up skin into folds which were meditative and inward turning as the mantle of a 14th century Madonna; then in a reversal that we experienced as a huge change from night to day, or the turning in some great argument, we brought our hands down. It made us gasp. The pace was excruciating. We were permanently aroused, erectile tissue flooded and damned up, and so we enjoyed a kind of leisure and Mozartian wit. I knew from the first with Brian that we would continue. Love and friendship aside, you can tell on a first meeting that it will take more exchanges to accomplish the various sexual permutations—know by the way he touches you rather than by positions and tastes.

I could just see the top of Brian's sunny head over the horizon of his chest. Silence, gasps—out of the blue he said, "You would have looked like dynamite in that toga."

What if I'm fucking on the grass in ancient Rome like we always do on Wednesday night. Is it Thursday? What's one day? Nothing—you turn around and it's dark, the tick and tock of day and night. What if I'm the woman? I'm languidly stretched out on the grass fanning myself with a spray of flowering myrtle. When he enters me I'm spread open as a moth, I'm all colors. What if I'm the guy when I feel someone on me and wham!—I've got a cock up my ass—I never saw the guy before and I *still* haven't seen him but I ride his cock—why not?—I'm riding it across a continent of skin. I feel like a sandwich, the pleasure's in the middle because no one has had or knows this much—I can't see, I'm bellowing and I start to come, it begins in my ass as a pinpoint of light a thousand miles away. I move closer to it with a religious sense of well-being and when I come I shout a little prayer—I shout *Je-Sus!*

What if I'm fucking this boy and his orgasm is so absolute it leaves me gasping. What if I'm watching the three of them calling on their gods and gasping their extravagance—their arms and legs, their skin filled with rosy orifices, they look like an anemone. First I'm the woman, then I'm the man, then I'm Catullus, then I'm an observer remembering a poem, the distance becoming erotic.

He's going to make us into a poem, I've heard better lines. What if he takes us to his villa and merely to pluck at my nipples he feeds me olives pickled in caraway, dormice dipped in honey and rolled in poppy seed, sausages, orioles seasoned with pepper, capons and sow bellies, blood pudding, Egyptian and Syrian dates, veal, little cakes, grapes, pickled beets, Spanish wine and hot honey, chickpeas and lupines, endless filberts, an apple, roast bear meat, soft cheese steeped in fresh wine, tripe hash, liver in pastry boats, oysters and hot buttered snails, pastry thrushes with raisin and nut stuffing, quinces with thorns stuck in them to resemble sea urchins, because I'm handsome.

Some people like sex, most men don't. What if I'm blowing him, I look up as he brings down a knife—I either die or don't die. I'm alone at night in bed, someone's moving silently up the stairs—this was to be a sexual rendezvous but instead he intends to wrap a wire around my neck. I don't die but my erection's gone. I must begin again: what if he puts his hand under my tunic, his finger up my ass and I squirm down on it, why not? My girl's laughing—dildos shaped like birds and fish. He's moaning *Nostra Lesbia, Lesbia illa, illa Lesbia*—what is this, Latin? This guy's obviously educated.

Orioles must be aphrodisiac or maybe it's the situation because all we want to do is fuck, we can't keep our clothes on, we go to it, showing off for him. I love how our eyes go blank and then we think with our bodies. She licks it like a cat with her rough tongue, or like licking ketchup off your forefinger—one two, that's all. Then men come and lift me and hold my legs and body while he fucks me and I'm blowing somebody, it's fantastic, all I ever want to do is this.

Brian and I were working ourselves around to coming; we enjoyed the sense of absolute well-being and safety that precedes orgasm. By now we were on our knees kissing urgently and masturbating ourselves. Our cocks felt a little ragged and wanted the master's touch. Masturbation can *feel* better, although I favor a penetration for emotional meaning. Still, that was hardly necessary since we filled up the house to overflowing, and besides, we weren't planning to have a baby.

Orgasms come in all shapes and sizes, sometimes mechanical as a jack-in-the-box—an obsessive little tune, tension, pop goes the weasel—other times they brim with meaning. And other times, like now, they are the complimentary close that signals the end of a lengthy exchange. I recall a memorable climax, a terrific taste of existence in the summer of '73. I was with Ed; we weren't doing anything special but the orgasm started clearly with the fluttering of my prostate, usually a distant gland, sending icy waves to my extremities. Then a hot rush carried my torso up into an arc and just before I came a ball bearing of energy ping-ponged up and down my spine.

Brian and I curled into each other. Our semen smelled faintly of chlorine. Sunlight glittered off or was accepted by the domestic surfaces. On our way to falling asleep we exchanged dreams:

Bob: I dreamt that an alligator lives in my kitchen wall; it cries brokenheartedly on the weekends. A cannibal rabbit with sharp teeth lives there too. A pathetic shabby man who looks like Genet keeps beckoning to me, appearing at a distance everywhere, even on the Greyhound bus I take to escape him, standing up the aisle and beckoning. These characters fill me with dread. I know they can't hurt me in themselves—they are intensely defeated, already claimed by death to such an extent that I writhe backward rather than associate with them.

Brian: I dreamt this while I was nuts. A group of nuns in black and white floated on the surface of a foreign planet. They were only heads, like that creature in the space movie. In their hands they carried candles that vibrated colors and gold. Everything on the nuns' side was grey and dead, but where the candles were, the light created moving patterns of color and electricity.

Bob: One day Denise, following a recipe of mine, made baked apples in wine. But something went awry and they turned out hard and sour. That night I dreamt there was a new kind of elephant called an Applederm, and its babies were called Apples.

Brian: I was at a party with my father. Our hosts—a family—were noticeably absent, which made me angrier and angrier. I followed my father into the dining room to placate myself with some food and as I looked up I realized it was my parents' apartment. There was laughter from the other room and someone said, "All our hearts are the same here."

Bob: I dreamt this around puberty. I was making love with my little sister on her bed but the springs squeaked and I was anxious because my family in the next room might hear us. So we became bumblebees and hovered above the bed, buzzing and buzzing, and when we touched stingers I came.

(I never told anyone my bumblebee dream, had forgotten it for years. I felt that now Brian could know me in one piece—what wasn't in the dream he could extrapolate.)

Brian: I stood in a room that was all black and white and because the dream was in color it was beautifully vivid. Black and white tiled floor, white walls, black and white solid drapes. As I looked around the room I saw a black bed from classical Greece, white sheets and in the bed a boy, sun-tanned with platinum blond hair. The contrast between him and the black and white setting filled me with joy; I moved closer passing through veils of black and white (remember duality?) and as I kissed him I awoke with the overwhelming erection that only dreams can provide.

Brian and I sometimes exchange letters. In the latest, Brian told me he is moving in with a lover. I felt a pang that I had no right to turn into any claim—the pain augmented by the fact that Sterling moved out of my life without leaving a forwarding address. I had been curious about the story Brian painted from his mother's childhood.

He answered: "The image was based on one of my mother's frequent outings with my grandmother, my Great-Aunt Kate and her Uncle Ollie. Kate's husband, Hugo, died young and on weekends my grandmother and Kate would pack a picnic and make a day of visiting Hugo. I'm not sure why this is so peculiar to me. Maybe because that's my mother's impression of it. More likely it's that Be-Be (our name for my grandmother) and Katie were so unaware of the irony of taking children to play in a cemetery. I made my mother the embracer and my uncle the observer. Later, Katie was institutionalized along with both her daughters, who somehow were not in on these trips. I met Katie when I was six and she would definitely win my most-terrifying-person-I-ever-met award. She had straight black hair cut severely across with straight long bangs. She sat hostilely on my grandmother's sofa, barely acknowledging our family's presence. She also scared the shit out of my father. She eventually died in a hospital singing Irish lullabies to herself.

"My grandmother held her own in the strange department. In her sixties she had to have one of her eyes—including the lid—removed. Instead of wearing a patch, Be-Be opted for glasses with a large plastic artificial eye attached to one of the lenses. It had a bizarre effect, particularly when she napped. What can I say about riding the subway with her—that people stared? that I got angry? It made me dislike people and love her. She would call and invite me to lunch. 'We'll go out!' she'd say expansively, as if The Acorn on Oak were the world. I gave her a feather boa one Christmas and we were thick as thieves after that. She loved to dance, drink. She would come out of the bathroom with hair she had just bleached platinum, make a 20's pout in the mirror, say, 'Your mother and I are both blonds,' and giggle. She was great.

"When Be-Be died, she presented a unique problem to the undertaker. My mother insisted that the coffin be open in the Irish tradition. The undertakers were perplexed—should they put Be-Be's glasses on her and create the disconcerting effect of a corpse with one eye open? In the end that's exactly what they did, and dressed in her favorite red beaded gown, Be-Be said goodbye.

"Moody in her earlier years, Be-Be became senile later. I'd go to her apartment and cook dinner. I loved her very much. In the hospital she suddenly became lucid and rose to the occasion of her death. She said, 'You always learn something. Now I'm learning about tenses. How long is this going to take?' Then she removed her rings, one by one, and placed them on the nightstand for my mother."

The Dinner Party

I FORGET THIS IS REALLY Southern California. You water, just water, and then a ferocious surge of greenery. I was checking the peach trees, overgrown with moss and curlicues of clematis—the giant peaches bunched and sometimes glowing with a nimbus of fruit flies where one had split open. It's hard to own up to beauty, to inhale and exhale it. Apples growing out of their flowers and strawberries rampant; the odor of mashed strawberries as I check the other side of the peach tree where I have to stand on a wall of cinderblocks. On one side, tireless growth. On the other, miles of shimmering asphalt. Always medieval to see passion flowers, and ivy up to the knee and magnolia gone wild—but the peach tree tame by now, every peach respectfully squeezed by me every day or so, so that I know the actual peaches and where three or four grow crowded into a grotto behind a clump of leaves. You wait and wait and then boom! it's peaches—not measured out but *all ready.*

For Mike, the peach tree's owner, the peaches are a problem and a responsibility. Mike said, "The turkey occupies a place in my life not unlike the peach tree." I was in the bathroom brushing my teeth and admiring the blue and white tile, and heard "future" for "peach tree" and thought, how apt—that certainly is the strong point and drawback of a turkey—you cook it up and then for the next amount of future, it's just turkey. It was dinner time. The candle melted into a Ludwig's castle. It was dark. I thought, Till age snow white haires on thee, Till age snow white haires on thee, Till age snow white haires on thee. It had caught my mind like a jingle. I liked the six stressed syllables in seven; I liked the comforting relationship it drew between my aging and natural history. It was written when nature was an active principle rather than a fond thought. On the other hand: Thou, when thou retorn'st, wilt tell mee All strange wonders that befell thee, And sweare No where Lives a women true, and faire.

True and fair. To let your hair become a rope ladder for the muscular repositioning of the arms and legs of just one hero. It's hard to be someone's radiant property and it's hard not to. Mike grew tired of being nice and satisfied himself with gentle insults. A difficult pause in the dinner conversation; people are edgy. Someone tells us about a black woman with a feather in her hat who stood in front of him at the bank. The woman said, "I've got shock in the eyeballs. I saw the neighbor boy, six or seven, playing in the car and I shouted NO but he rolled backwards across the street. I saw it all and since then I have headaches in my eyes and the doctor says I've got shock in my eyeballs, shock in my eyeballs." And someone else tells about walking up Third in New York when a dog ran into traffic and a woman grabbed her little boy, covered his eyes and yelled DON'T LOOK with a shout that practically took the back of his head off. Smart lady, they all agree. They are edgy. Everyone wants everything to be nice but nothing will ever stay in place. None of our lives occurs two or three or many times in the restful way they should, like national holidays. We are filled with this longing larger than a goal or object. What if we said in unison, "Oh I miss you and am lonely for you," with the understanding that no one knows who the you is. The world wants to intrude. A forlorn pause. Thorns begin to creep over the silence.

I smile beautifully at the man on my right. I remind him of a few things: smell of a sheepskin coat, syrup bleeding through the paraffin in a jar of marmalade that gleams drunkenly, holiday baking odors resonant and chaste, after sex watching *Mildred Pierce* on TV, walking the dog at two a.m. in the stately night—the beautiful hour of too many at two in the morning when disordered excitement is measured against the strictness of fatigue. There's a whole life like waxing the car on Father's Day, fireflies heightening our being, and the losers weepers' sweetness of "putting the kids to bed"—our impressionist melons and "Grande Jattes, "as though we had a past (and now we are safe and memory bittersweetly invades the harrowed border of a decade). And surely we are all sensitive and thoughtlessly treasure a few objects in our homes like a blue and white Imari sake cup or souvenirs from nature. I indicate the distracting beauties on the table, Jamesian, tame, abundant. Spread out between the Limoges and the silver are *crudités,* Cornish game hens with oyster dressing, red German cabbage, little peas and pearl onions, new potatoes tossed in butter and parsley, a casserole of Brussels sprouts with leeks and chestnuts, the wines. The soup was carried out. The salad comes later. Then coffee and cranberry soufflé and we will fill the moat and pull up the drawbridge on a safe life.

a safe life

a family life

everyone's the same as we are

ferocious life

six jacks and a ball life

wrapped boxes from U.P.S.

suffering can make us two-dimensional as well as resonant

spectacular life, as in "The highest degree of illusion comes to be the highest degree of sacredness." Feuerbach cited by Guy Debord

The curves in my rocking-chair life

colonized Third World gods

polite smile waiting to burst into fraud (the smile shaped like a canoe going elsewhere)

somehow I don't feel right unless I have a chicken in the freezer life

polite questions, knowledge is power

Sabatier, Henckels and Solingen

"We were poor and could not afford for her the soil of easy growth." Tillie Olsen

Toothbrush, bathmat, toilet paper, underwear, silverware, socks, towels, eyeglasses, jewelry and everything that touches

sex is OK but don't talk about money

children turning sundials — I mean cartwheels

upholstered life

A life beyond conflict with list upon list upon list upon list, as lists say commodity even when we number our sorrows and count our blessings. What form can that life and this story take but unwilling parody, because the desire to own and be owned subjects us to an envy which, compounded by powerlessness, dissolves us in recurrent daydreams. So myself in the form of a husband or father tells Mike that he may not leave the table until all his liver is gone. And strange I think to myself, still smiling, how strange it seems to me that two of my gracious guests are quarreling about who has to do the dishes. They keep whining subnormally: "No fair" and "Gonna tell on you." I think I'll blink a few times to see if that will change something. Myself as the husband is really furious; he's shouting at Mike, "Eat it or wear it, eat it or wear it, eat it or wear it." Poor Mike is gagging. I smile ferociously at the man on my right, *"Would you care for more peas?"* Sometimes a person's tongue becomes a whole dining room table tasting, and that's not bad. Still, a person could lay down the fork and say, "Is this to my benefit?" Mike is submerged in a crying so convulsed that the room and the rest of the world look strangely flat, and other betrayals we forgot or censored are recalled at the deepest point because the crying makes a bridge. We think of our good points, our intelligent eyes and the arc our lives can make toward a human future. We feel sleepy because it's night and it's restful to know who and what our enemies and friends are.

CHAUCER

WALKING WITH MY BROTHER down Hollywood Boulevard;
it's Friday and everyone's made of flesh and selling this
and that, addicted. Walking at night, filled with our lives,
everything seems sadly possible. At the Bijou, Pasolini's
Canterbury Tales:

THE PARDONER'S PROLOGUE

A garish carrousel horse suspended above a store
entrance. In this story treasure is not three wishes, expression
of eternal optimism—it's money. The Pardoner gives us his
terms from the start: I file my tongue and make ideas work
for me—the only professional storyteller among us—selling a
story and a lot of trash passed off as relics: pieces of saints that
are pig bones and sheep bones, a pillowcase that is Mary's
veil, rubbish and dirt. I'm a good talker, it's a good story, one
of those chilling medieval parables. I didn't make up the story
or the ideology. I'm that merry-go-round horse. People like it.
I carry them in.

THE PARDONER'S TALE

There are three men.

How good looking they are:

The gliding muscles of historical flesh. 14th century daylight plays on their flesh framed by an historical keyhole, rib cage and the bird in that pie; 14th century light sketching an elbow, a hip, sending an instep into darkness. Still, it's more believable to say rough trade in Flanders. The more you describe, the less credible, because your labor distracts everyone. Science fiction likes minute descriptions to win our acknowledgment. If you try that tactic on a cup of coffee, like Robbe-Grillet, the pressure forces the cup's existence into question, like saying a word over and over till it turns to mud that makes a logjam of possible actions: world world world world world world.

So there are three sitting in a tavern that tips off its center of gravity. They enjoy the company of the loudmouthed, the flatterers, the mock-modest, the faultfinders, gossips, rioters and gamblers, tittle-tattlers, talebearers and every kind of grumbler. They jolt one shiftless celebration into the next and stay drunk. One of them killed Pasolini. Six red eyes above a cupped hand that shelters a match.

A corpse goes by. Our friend died, his death carried around on the tone of a bell. Let's avenge our friend; we'll find Death and kill him. They swear to be friends but it's obvious that a scrap of the least gristle would make a dogfight. Last night I went to a reading and the poets were dinosaurs showing off their ice age and then going out for a beer and slapping each other on the back and slamming their fists on the table. In whatever likeness the fiend appears he has never more than one nostril, which is great and wide, and he will gladly turn it up so that we can see through to his brain. And his brain is nothing else than the fire of hell, for the fiend cannot have any other brain. I could tell you their names but you know them, their initials go A to Z.

These men set out to find Death. They walk down a clean dirt road brushing flies away, they are innocent, they tell each other jokes: What did one peanut say to the other peanut while walking in the park? I was *a-salted*. Ha Ha Ha, Oh ha ha ha.

Why is an elephant's foot a sexual object? Cause if it steps on you you're *fucked*.

Oh ha ha ha—lurching over,

Oh by the Cross, by the Thorns, by the Blood, Nails and Thorns, Bones and Blood!

They've heard these jokes a hundred times so they start laughing at the first few words, becoming flirtatious out of hilarity, calling the youngest "Little Pie Legs" and "Little Sausage Fingers," goosing him, "You like to pitch or catch?"

Three cardinals and three blackbirds display their technique, singing roundelays, sestinas, sonnets, ballads, any cute thing you can imagine,

Her skirt was of the grass green silk
Her mantle of the velvet fine
At each lock of her horse's mane
Hung fifty silver bells and nine,

then come to rest on a mulberry branch, six in a row, red black red black red black, their beaks to the south, their eyes to the

71

east and west. They just weathered the Hundred Years War, the Black Death and the Peasants' Revolt—Her skirt was of the grass green silk—so they sing a literature of dreams.

The Pardoner says, "Folks, you give me your money and I'll absolve you of your personality." Laughter and applause.

About half a mile and they meet an old man; the folds of his mantle fall like straight rain. He's not just an old man, he's the prototype, familiar and hyperreal. He wants to die and calls the earth his mother. He lives in a kinder, an older world than the three who berate him. The earth is my mother and I knock with my staff on the ground, my mother's gate, and say, "Mother, let me in." He understands along with the Pardoner the new thing, the power of abstraction in the form of money. He says in rhymes:

> The most important phenomenon of the later
> Thirteenth and the Fourteenth to an able spectator
> In England, is the gradual and sporadic
> Reduction of land-bound serfs, and the traumatic
> Emergence of a group of laborers, unlanded
> And working for wages, such as yourself.
> Page One of a candid
> Mystery whose detective waits five ratty
> Centuries away. The dark freedom to move
>   from Cincinnati
> To LA for higher wages in a new city
> Is the same that creates our dark interiority.

The old man says Death is waiting for them up a crooked path in a grove under an oak tree; he points. The three set out to find Death instead of three people to love their actual bodies in expansive sexual play. They find money—a play of light on the coins: We're rich! How much is it? Count it, Ass-face! No more working and fasting, eating crackers and shit, weak drinks at the Bow-Wow Club, taking orders, no more cold, loneliness, terror, lice, insecurity, yes sir, no sir, skin infections, malnutrition—which translates to eight bushels of florins. They think of hot marrow trickling down their throats, spices from leaves bark and roots seasoning a sauce, red and white wine, cooks stamping and straining and grinding.

These guys never had a chance. When they thought death was an abstraction, who would tell them otherwise—the priest? the innkeeper? In this story only the Pardoner has access to that knowledge. See how corrupt it all is? He says, "And wouldn't a person forget about death, isn't that the idea, to grow abstract?—to separate the body and the mind?" A *New Yorker* cartoon shows the Grim Reaper standing before the president of the corporation's desk. What a localized surprise; from the great height of his position the president barks, "Who the hell are you? And how did you get past Miss Merryweather?" Money makes Miss Merryweather's life abstract too, but less precious. Sold in chunks. Hollywood Boulevard. I felt depressed. That's why I described these afflicted relationships with such splendor and fatality to my brother, who had already witnessed so much. I observed the splendor of it. This story can come to no good, I thought enthusiastically. For this to be over, for that to be over, for everybody's everything to be finished—*who cares?* Throw out the mental hopechests and scrapbooks and telephone directories so that each one is alone—the corrosive irony of separation. A solitary figure chased across a TV screen: we are supposed to relax into this image. The plot hones itself, it's irrelevant; crude background music carries us over tough chaparral or down city canyons. The attraction is a person without allies. Everything drops away from him including the unity of the world. Take Bruce's upstairs neighbor, Mrs. Hazel Scrivani. The landlord spelled her name Scravini on the mailbox the first day she moved in and it's stayed that way for sixteen years. *"Oh well, it's only my name, my time and my life."*

Suddenly the world with all its East West North and South became that money. We'll wait until dark and carry it back. You go for bread and wine, we'll guard it. The youngest goes for the food, puts rat poison in the wine. The two remaining agree to kill him and divide the cash two ways. They pretend to struggle with him—just a game—then knife him in the heart; then they drink: their throats become sewers: they die. So food and play are the vehicles for their death.

Their death: I don't want to fill up the landscape with it. When it came to dying theirs was as particular as yours and mine: no more regrouping, no making plans.

NIGHT FLIGHT

A CEILING OF LOW CLOUDS domesticates the light, slanting and yellowing it. A promise of rain. That interior light brings distant and near into sharp focus, makes the stop sign, telephone pole, the bland pueblo-faced building across the street and the hills beyond—makes them accurate, brings them to a point. Lily jumps on my bed to put herself in the path of some affection, curls into her tail and dozes off. Then the twilight gives its intensity to the streetlights while my house fills with the sweet metallic artichoke scent—smell rather—the artichoke intact in its steamer suffering a medieval torture.

Bruce and I spent a strange afternoon. He wanted a black leather jacket. Denise, myself and other friends approved of his decision and Bruce's ex-lover viewed it a little anxiously, which seemed propitious. Bruce rarely buys anything, fearing that one purchase will lead to the next and so on—like S/M where you must always raise the ante to achieve the same degree of pleasure until you become a different person and not necessarily the one you intended. If I am an image for myself and other people, why not name the pleasure of manipulating that image? I love the world's merchandise. I love bins heaped with pippins or Gravensteins, abstruse cookware, the exotic and familiar shapes of antiques, drastic white sales where saleswomen call me honey and hum "Love is Blue," plush haberdasheries with salesmen superior and groveling like waiters in fine French restaurants, and I can vouch for the accuracy of Bruce's line of thought.

We prefaced our afternoon with lunch at a cafe on Polk Street. Bruce chose it. He pointed out the good bread, big soups and salads—I could see he wanted me to like it. It was Jewish-organic—to my surprise I did like it. I ordered a whole wheat bagel with fresh cream cheese and a cold fruit soup tasting of apricots and cinnamon. Bruce had some cosmopolitan mix of avocado, sprouts, pocketbread, cream cheese and green chilies. We settled in, obligingly gauging ourselves to each other's rhythm as a sign of friendship: my abbreviations and wisecracking, Bruce's paragraphs and meditative periods.

I thought, "I haven't been remembering my dreams," and with that my morning dream returned. I told it to Bruce. I dreamed I was dying. I cheerfully move beneath the vast dome of a hospital—the ceiling speeds and gleams like the inverted jewelry of a tape recorder. I walk up to a man suspended from the ceiling by his veins and arteries who tells me the meaning of life (which I forget) and then teaches me how to resurrect. (We avert our eyes even in dreams—even when I shut them I see a horizon line.) I returned to life but then I went back and dreamed I died and stayed put. The bottom of the first dream gently gave way and the following dream occurred in its basement. I'm walking through a factory in the beautiful collective future of 2050. I'm in charge of converting matter into energy. I simply chuck matter through a porthole, a cool blue light spangles from inside and then a city has enough power. I feel a pleasurable impulse to put parts of my body through the window. It's slightly forbidden and intensely exciting. I start inconspicuously: little toe, little finger. Finally I ease in my whole body—a sensual rush—synapses diffusing—ejaculation.

I began enthusiastically but as I said my dream out loud I grew more and more forlorn. We changed the subject to the Left Writers Union that Bruce and I helped found. It was in trouble—letters of outrage flew back and forth like killer bees. Bruce wanted stories about the union for his next book, particularly stories about Jack Hirschman the "Poet Laureate of the Left." Jack remained cheerfully impervious to the sexual politics of the last twenty years. He worked with us on "Left/Write," a large writing conference, and I reminded Bruce about the time Jack, in the spirit of proletarian unity, addressed Denise, the planning committee and History with his extended arms and majestic voice, "But dear, we're *all* black lesbians!"—to which Denise (straight and white) replied very evenly, "Jack, if I ever hear you say that again I'm going to kill you." I added that I was not present; I heard the story second, no, third hand—while the incident grew doubtful its emotional life remained surprisingly unhampered. Then I reported to Bruce that a local poet called me a Stalinist. We laughed, raising our eyebrows at a breathtaking vista of wrongheadedness. Bruce drew back as though Gloria Vanderbilt had invited me to a yachting weekend; he protested, "But *I* wanted to be the one who's denounced!" We decided that when we seize power we will not send that poet to a reeducation camp in Siberia, but to charm school.

Then I launched into my lovelorn complaint about Felix. I had bestowed my heart far off; Felix already lived with a man and "he didn't even know I existed." My lament bored even myself since it was all feeling and no real information, no plot at all. Depression made me tedious and repetitive. Words failed me: all morning a stale moronic voice had mentally shouted, "Surely the borders are dusty and dirty, thought Gerty, but that's the nature of tried and true. Mostly the larder is musty and fusty, thought Rusty, a cat's a watcher a slide rule too. Surely Gerty is crusty and rusty, thought Bertie...." That alternated with a stanza I dreamed years ago which sometimes catches hold like a persistent tune:

> Cardiovascular destiny
> Or, uh, fate
> Makes Tony stony angry
> So he won't capitulate.

I still don't understand the point of this sorrow—Felix is shorthand for a yearning too big to name. *A stifled, drowsy, unimpassioned grief*: it presents itself as a puzzle: a feeling with no outlet. At its worst, I struggle to remember a melody playing just beyond my grasp. That lost music would unite meaning and incident—would give this mystery a plot.

A makeshift solution—I borrow a plot from Sade:
Having had nothing but unpleasantness from my first lover, who long ago abandoned me in order to throw himself into a life of debauchery, and being obliged to assume that this creature is in his grave (if I shoved sand down a rat hole for a decade it's not the rat's fault but am I supposed to love it?)—I began contemplating the idea of again taking a lover; this time a sensible man who, by the kindness of his character and the excellence of his morals, would make me forget my earlier mishaps. My first lover bore two children: a boy

who died early, and another boy who, at the age of fifteen, abandoned me as my lover had done, in order to pursue the same licentious ways. I have an income of $20,000 a year.

A former colleague said: "The man I'm proposing to you was raised by Mr. Saint-Prat, a reputable man who gives him $10,000 a year. Felix is thirty-six but he looks no more than twenty-eight. Pleasing face, skin/lily, soft brown hair, mouth/ rose, excellent figure, graceful movements, extremely pious, conscientious in his monastery duties, enchants everyone, angel on earth."

When I saw Felix I loved him: lily, rose, graceful. He looked like me and when he didn't know people, he also thought of them as strangers.

He said: Bob, you haven't been told everything. I can't be your lover without giving you a chance to judge whether or not I'm worthy of it. My family is unknown to me. I was found in a green taffeta bassinet on the Saint-Prats' doorstep. Since there was no indication of my name, it pleased Mrs. Saint-Prat to name me Felix. I had just reached the age of fifteen when I had the misfortune of seeing my foster mother die. Mr. Saint-Prat made it clear to me that I could no longer stay in his house. "I'm a widower and still young," that virtuous man said to me. "If you and I were to live under the same roof now, it would give rise to doubts which we don't deserve. I have a widowed sister, I'm going to send you to her."

In Mrs. Verquin's house, frivolity, independence and the pursuit of pleasure were enthroned, and the impure air I breathed began to pollute my soul. As soon as a charming and witty young man, Senneval, told me of his love for me, I felt irresistibly drawn to him. We resembled each other and we were so attracted that even when we sat at different tables in a restaurant there was a fucking motion between us. As you know, pleasure deposes anxiety, the two can't exist side by side. Mrs. Verquin assured me that I could receive my lover in her house every night without fear. I wanted to fly behind him as he approached — put my palms against his calves so I could be where the muscle accepts his weight. He made love to me as though I were a mirror. He drew his head back and made his lips quiver, then thrust his tongue deep into my mouth as though a mirror were watching him there too. I became pregnant. I nearly died of despair when I discovered my condition. I gave birth to a boy. Senneval begged me to leave his son to him. He placed the child in a country house where it was impossible for me to find him. What a credulous fool I was! I hadn't believed that a man could amuse himself by seducing an unfortunate boy and then abandoning him. He left; he tore himself away from my breast wet with my tears *without shedding a single tear of his own.*

Mr. Saint-Prat suggested that I go live with one of his other relatives, a woman famous for her lofty piety. Mrs. Lerince accepted me gladly. In her house sexuality was a drawer with a key. I won't bore you with the monotonous details of my life during the seventeen years I was fortunate enough to live with that adorable woman. Then Saint-Ange appeared. Everyone was rather uneasy about our lack of knowledge of this young man. He had a handsome face, worthy of an artist's brush. Bob, whether from a presentiment or any other reason you may care to name, as soon as I saw that young face I began to tremble all over without being able to determine the cause. A similar reaction had also taken place in him, as he later told me himself. "Really, Saint-Ange," I said to him, "you must have a false idea of your worth or else you have time to waste since you spend it with a man twice your age." He replied, "Hate me, traitor, hate me, since that's my unhappy fate, but never hope to overcome the love for you with which I'm burning...." I wanted to cover my nipples with my palms and run away on eighth-note legs, shouting no-no-no-no-no in falsetto. "Alas," I said to myself, "he's the image of Senneval, who spoke to me in the same way... and also in a garden, a garden like this one!"

Since it was a very hot night, I lay down on my bed almost naked. My eyes had scarcely begun to close when I heard a sound... I felt a hand seize me. It was Saint-Ange. "Infamous seducer!" I cried. That ardent young man threw himself on me so skillfully and in such a state of frenzy that I became his victim before I was able to do anything to prevent it. He shuffled and reshuffled my body; I flew through his hands like a card trick. Then I broke away and snatched up the scissors that were lying at my feet. "Traitor!" I cried, stabbing what I thought was his arm. Good heavens! I had stabbed him through the heart! I threw myself on his bloody body and feverishly clasped it to my agitated breast... I pressed my mouth to his.

Felix broke off his narrative because of the tears that were choking him. He lay down on the floor, saying, "I cry easier on a hard surface." I averted my eyes to keep him from feeling like a biological specimen in my sharper focus. "Be calm," I said. "It was a terrible misfortune, but there's not even the shadow of a crime in that fatal event. The sternest tribunal would do nothing except wipe away your tears."

Felix said: Let me go on. Crushed by this catastrophe, I wrote to Mr. Saint-Prat. I decided to rest for a time at an inn, waiting for his reply. One evening as I was about to go into my chamber, a man in his early fifties suddenly came out of his room and, armed with a dagger, rushed into a room across the hall. I hurried forward, and before I had time to stop him or even call out to him, I saw that wretched man throw himself on another man and stab him in the heart a dozen times. The murderer was imprisoned, but he admitted nothing and firmly maintained that he was innocent. I was the only witness, I had to speak. I would have given anything to avoid that cruel testimony, especially against a man with whom I shared a striking physical likeness. The next morning, that miserable man was put to death.

On that same day I received Mr. Saint-Prat's answer. He urged me to come back. I asked him to find me a retreat in which I could end my days in the deepest solitude and in the most rigorous duties of my religion. He suggested the one in which you found me.

By the time he had ended his story, Felix was in a state of violent agitation. I did not feel that the later events presented any more valid reasons for changing my plans than the earlier ones had done. I did everything I could to calm the man I loved. "Felix," I said, "let's conclude our arrangements, I beg you, and let me convince you that there's nothing in your story that could diminish, in the heart of an honest man, either the consideration owed to all your virtues or the homage demanded by all your charms."

Mr. Saint-Prat doubled Felix's income to $20,000 a year and bequeathed us $100,000. Felix and I had spent nearly three months together, and we were already certain of his pregnancy, when an unexpected event blighted our wellbeing and changed our tender roses into the mournful cypresses of sorrow.

Felix was standing beside me, about seven o'clock on an October evening, reading a gloomy English novel. A lilac colored servant came in to say that a stranger was insistently asking to speak to me. Felix shuddered. That shudder was a sentinel. Involuntary tears streamed down my lover's cheeks, his legs became unsteady and he sat down; he tried to speak, but even his voice died on his lips—"It's nothing, Bob, nothing.... Let the gentleman come in."

"Father!" cried the stranger, throwing himself at my feet. He said:

"Will you recognize a wretched son who's been separated from you for twenty-two years? Please sit down and hear me—my story is like two or three heartbeats.

"I left you when I was fifteen. My first impulse was to go to my mother, but his scandalous life alarmed me so much that I had to flee. When I was seventeen I fell in love with Mrs. Verquin's young protege, but in pursuing such beauty there is always a feeling of being left behind. I seduced him, had a son by him, then cruelly abandoned him. I won't describe the mishaps I encountered after that; they were countless. Meanwhile my son grew and showed great promise. But he fell in love with a charming man. One night my son tried to take by force what the man refused him out of virtue. Intending only to frighten my son, the man stabbed him with a scissors, but they pierced his heart and he fell dead....

"I traveled. When I arrived at a certain inn I learned that a Mr. Desbarres—this was the name my mother had adopted—had just been imprisoned for having stabbed his rival to death. A man who happened to be in the inn saw the murder; his testimony was the sole cause of my mother's sentence. I asked to see my mother and my request was granted. He told me, 'As soon as my eyes are closed, go to Bob and tell him that among my crimes there's one which he never knew. Senneval, you have a brother. 'I decided to get rid of him. I resolved to kill him, but my wet nurse told me that she knew of a man who wanted children. My son was left on the doorstep of that man, whose name is Mr. Saint-Prat, in a green taffeta bassinet."

Senneval ended his story. I was deeply perturbed, all my senses were frozen, I nearly lost consciousness. I thought, "If you can't touch someone you can't touch him, not with the good you can do or the harm." Felix had been torn to pieces for the last quarter of an hour. He said, "Well, Bob, now do you believe that a more horrible criminal than the wretched Felix exists anywhere in the world? Recognize me, Senneval, recognize me as your brother, recognize me as the boy you seduced, your son's murderer, our father's lover, and the infamous creature who led our mother to the scaffold!"

About three months ago I saw a young man at a restaurant. I say young man. Later I learned that he is twenty-eight but his forehead is high and his neck is thin so he'll always look a little like an eighth grader. He is about my height with very fine features of the lengthened sort. He has soft, dark hair. His nostrils are fine, though a little painful—his mouth is bad and good. His profile is better than his full face; his movements are very graceful. I pointed him out to Denise, remarking how appealing he was—so soft and serious, so palatable, the adolescence of a nectarine. Denise replied that of course I liked his looks, he looked like me! She was right but not in any particular way—a general rosy paleness, a quiet manner, something—it made me feel as though we corresponded. I wanted to wrap him in tenderness. It happened that we had mutual friends, that he is the lover of one of them, and I was to see him in the most constrained way. Desire made me self-conscious. I couldn't look at him or talk to him.

Bruce suggested that perhaps I didn't crave Felix as much as I let on. He listed Felix's drawbacks, physical and spiritual. I reminded Bruce that Felix resembled me. Still, I agreed that my urgency could be loneliness stepped-up to a pitch. Felix defines my isolation and my pleasure. Lately when I see someone attractive I don't think about sex, I wonder how it would be to watch TV together, bake him coffee cake. Sleeping alone takes on more meaning every day—it gains momentum so that I'm afraid it will grow too commanding to resist. (Isolation scares me in that it becomes workable, a *modus operandi*.) It's like factoring in more and more of my death. I quoted a favorite passage from Dear Abby. "The grief and loneliness of being left alone make us hunger for something we can hardly define. Signed, Alone and Lonely."

I reminded Bruce of the new *Semiotext(e)*. The issue's theme is "Polysexuality." On the front cover, in color, a beefcake scowls on a motorcycle. He has a massive naked ass, huge belligerent thighs; he wears a black leather cap, black leather vest, boots and nothing else—the Man. On the back cover a dead man in black and white slumps on a grubby toilet. He wears only high heels and garters (the Woman?) and it looks like everything terrible has been done to him—charred flesh, edema from tight ropes, knife wounds, all brutally reflected in a bathroom mirror. The figure's isolation in death, magnified by the mirror, frightened me more than the squalidness and brutality. Bruce caught my drift, suggesting that modern life provides its residents with a sexuality whose private nature can lead to a death frightening in its sordidness and isolation. Let that describe my solitude as a pretext to show it to you, a pretext to colonize some outpost of interior life with the ferocity of an army of names. Bruce compared the *Semiotext(e)* cover with the Aztec passage in my "Sex Story," which shows semi-naked priests killing a naked man in a ritual. The isolation of the *Semiotext(e)* death and the ceremony of the other are objective facts in the two societies. The public aspect of the Aztec death confers a meaning we can hardly imagine but the magazine image belongs to us; it's the crown and scepter of our exiled sexuality, expressing a loneliness so ingrained that we don't have a language to speak of its opposite. Until death has a socialized meaning we substitute an interiorized experience, distorted and feverish—it bursts out of our sliver of a body as a gorgeously ugly flower.

I say, "I could wish no one but myself knew you had ever existed." What good is identity if it doesn't equal the world? Felix mock bows, replies, "I see you through a Mist—as I dare say you do me by this time. You are my judge: my forehead is on the ground. As far as they regard myself I can despise all events: but I cannot cease to love you." As he bows the linen irritates his nipples into semierection and his rib cage, hung for a second from his bent spine, reveals its whole self. (A fleeting notion of his death and I am washed with tenderness for him and a longing for harmony.) As he bows his penis retracts and the crack of his ass lengthens—no, I don't have him naked now. I take his worried smile, his seriousness which I *grow* to love. I say, "All my thoughts, my unhappiest days and nights have I find not at all cured me of my love of Beauty, but made it so intense (when we walk down the street I arrange for his shadow to fall on my skin) that I am miserable when you are not with me (when he leaves I fold myself in his blankets to wrap his smell around me and cry from excess): or rather breathe in that dull sort of patience that cannot be called Life. I never knew before what such a love as you have made me feel, was; I did not believe in it; my Fancy was afraid of it, lest it should burn me up. But if you will fully love me, though there be some fire, 'twill not be more than we can bear when moistened and bedewed with Pleasure." Felix climbs on the bed. This language amuses him (an ironic smile) and he also believes it (an erection). He runs a finger along a vein on my belly and whispers, "I cannot conceive of any beginning of such love as you have for me but Beauty. Write the softest words and kiss them that I may touch my lips where yours have been." His lips become dry and filled out; a tongue, alarmingly large and frank, rests between those lips. It's my birthday—I unravel the ribbons, open the lid—OH MY GOD it's a big copper tin-lined cordon bleu oval casserole with brass handles and beaten sides, estimated price $250-275 (unless he found it on sale?). Tears stream down my face—I love it! Now I know he really loves me—it's like signing a contract! I dreamt Felix's naked torso floats next to me at waist level. I tremble in my urge and distress, urge and fear; I dare to run my hand across his white skin which is a light source, skirting over his ribs to the soft belly. I say, "I have two luxuries to brood over in my walks, your Loveliness and the hour of my death. O that I could have possession of them both in the same minute. I hate the world: it batters too much the wings of my self-will, and would I could take a sweet poison from your lips to send me out of it." Is it just that one extremity suggests another? "Ask yourself my love whether you are not very cruel to have so entrammeled me, so destroyed my freedom."

I like the brown study aspect of this musing but what happens when we push it into action? I push him and his helpless thrashing only delights me more. It also delights him and suddenly he releases a hard shower of kisses. A mutual friend says Felix is very responsive in bed, testifying to his essential *creaminess,* so I interpolate half-sighs, a body that moves toward my hands. Felix knows sex as a mechanical science in which a libido is dutifully emptied by orgasms, like bailing water out of a leaky dinghy, so I present myself as a person with the *ability* to love. "I am indeed astonished to find myself so careless of all charms but yours—remembering as I do the time when even a bit of ribbon was a matter of interest with me. What softer words can I find for you after this—I am distracted with a thousand thoughts. I will imagine you Venus tonight and pray, pray, pray to your star like a Heathen." He is splayed on top of me—I push two fingers in his asshole, he pushes back in agreement—my fingers slowly turn on my wrist's axle—he feels his insides revolve (think of cosmologies)—he wallows, tongue out, eyes half shut—his head wants to rotate with my hand—there's nothing for him to do but moan and lick my instep like a dog. Smell is the sense absent from fantasy but he looks like spearmint. I call your attention to these removes because I'm not a salon artist who applies brown glaze to his canvas so that it blends with the rest of the museum. I used to memorize Keats's poems and write them out pretending they were mine—lacking both an object and language and yet needing a future. The language of romance is not ours—only by naming its distant, exotic quality can I use it. While I muse backward at Keats's landscape, look at how it appears in front of me again when S/M says: I am your prisoner, and, I would die for you, and, I am chained by your love, and "I cannot breathe without you," and, "I have a sensation at the present moment as though I was dissolving—I have been astonished that men could die Martyrs for religion—I shudder'd at it. I shudder no more— I could be martyr'd for my religion—Love is my Religion. I could die for that. I could die for you. My creed is love and you are its only tenet. You have ravish'd me away by a Power I cannot resist." Felix replies, "You must be mine to die upon the rack if I want you. I wish you could know the Tenderness with which I continually brood over your different aspects of countenance, action and dress." Felix licks the corners of my mouth, then asks the right questions so I can give the right answers and be naked. In this way we keep returning to each other, our faces filled with distance. Then we unfurl a communion so high that instead of speaking our tongues merely touch. My wish has long been that his very name could be forgotten by everyone but myself.

Bruce and I had grown meditative, imagining a time when power, love, friendship, beauty, sex and death will be facets of one experience rather than shattered fragments. I felt an urge to toss up all these pieces to see how they would fall. We left the restaurant and drove across town to Leather Forever, a store off Castro Street. On the way, Bruce paged through a Frank Frazetta comic book. Driving down Gough, two girls in pinafores waved from the bed of a pickup. It was almost raining—their hair whipped around and their eyes stayed wide open like archaic Greeks. Like the Korai, their gaze suggested enormous focus. The air resonated with wind and moisture; from sheer vividness they wore fixed smiles, and their waists and limbs were alert and physical. When I waved back a profound hilarity reduced them. One threw her eyes up in an excess of amusement and knotted her hands against her crotch. The other, totally undone, hid her face in her friend's neck. The hilarity was catching; I laughed and a thin wire of delight wiggled in my groin.

The store smelled smooth and seasoned, perfumed by the aisles of leather. Bruce and I collected some likely jackets and carried them back to the full length mirror. For a startled moment I caught our reflection before I was ready. My smile remained on my face like a photograph. I saw two men who looked a little rumpled and shy. They were in the middle of their lives; each one's particular old age waited patiently in his face. With a pang I saw that they were not beautiful, being more or less than their reflections. Bruce and I seemed united in this aging as though we were coconspirators in some adventure. I felt a welling up of tenderness for us. I wanted to cleave to Bruce and to the treasure of our friendship, achieved and reconciled.

My story begins with light and ends with the body. Bruce tried on one of the jackets and something surprising happened. The jacket was beautifully made. The Mongolian lamb, buttery and yielding, said touch me. 'Tis midnight, but small thoughts have I of sleep: The black looked deep and rich but its statement was power—death if you prefer—saying don't touch me: a mixed message at the heart of glamor. Full seldom *may my friend such vigils keep!* Certainly Bruce is a handsome man. Tall, slender, fine featured as a lemur. The black lent intention to his grizzled black hair and slate blue eyes. *Visit him, gentle Sleep! with wings of healing.* It heightened his tan, his good skin. It drew a frame around his handsomeness and advertised its availability. *And may this storm be but a mountain birth.* The addition of power rerouted the tenderness I already felt for Bruce. Bruce became a sexual object and the new direction was sexual appreciation. *May all the stars hang bright above his dwelling.* I encouraged him to buy the jacket.

VIOLENCE

DENISE AND I SAT at her kitchen table, talking about this
and that and drinking Mexican chocolate. "It has a funny
flavor," she said. I replied, "Ground almonds." Denise wore
her calico nightgown and pink velour robe. It was the kind
of social encounter I love, soft textures, sweet tastes. We had
just watched the last twenty minutes of a dopey little made-
for-TV horror movie about a beautiful house which loves its
owner, Debbie, so much that it will kill her and her boyfriend,
Frank, rather than let them leave. In one scene it knocks an old
woman into the swimming pool and boils her to death. The
governing personality belongs to the house which is sunny,
cheerfully LA modern—a variation on the house-as-monster
theme. I said, "If we asked Central Casting for the best actor to
play Personality don't you think they'd send us this house?"
Denise replied that perhaps for Personality something with
many tentacles might be nice, a hodgepodge, looking a bit
thrown together, say, an over-accesorized Japanese sci-fi
colossus, each adjustment to monster life a novelty: "It travels
under water on shark fins and propeller," said Denise; "Flies
with bat wings and jet engines," I added; "Shoots missiles and
lasers from its fingertips," she continued. We saw it heavy

with anxiety and destruction but without suspense. Or King Kong, a bull in a china shop. Meanwhile, Debbie stands in the driveway pleading with the house, "If you really, really love me, you'll let me go," and the house withdraws its hold, unraveling the thick security chain that is strangling Frank. The End.

I just dropped by to smoke a few of Denise's cigarettes and borrow her electric typewriter in order to put the finishing touches on my sex story. Our friendship has a lot of give. I talked about the change in direction my project had taken. *Elements* began as a prose series of shortish "pieces." Saying nothing is the best way to elude censorship—I fretted over abandoned scenes, whole areas, words. In the end I wanted a full-blooded recounting and an audience to hear it. Denise and I counted manuscript pages and came up with too few. *Elements* would make a slim volume but I didn't want it to be anemic. "What did I leave out?" I asked Denise. "I have sex, power and romantic love—that's Brian. I have politics and filial love—that's Bruce. 'Chaucer' is art, the 'Dinner Party' is Los Angeles. What's missing?" Denise answered, "Violence." "Violence," I said to myself, "that's Ed."

The next day I asked Ed what he thought of appearing in a story about violence. "Violence?" Forgetting his cake, he put down his fork and sat back. "No, that's just right. I feel like the world's exploding every second; if I close my eyes I see a giant meteor skirt Oakland and Berkeley." By way of example, he closed his eyes. Instead of trying to guess what transpired beneath those almond lids, I took the opportunity to enjoy his face at rest—sleek, high-colored as a cloisonné earring. I had watched him sleeping this way but that was years ago. I figured he said Oakland and Berkeley to allow distance for a good view—vast winds, city towers carried aloft, oranges and pinks of dazzling purity, all of it unfocusing binarily for an instant before exploding, too hot for flame. I asked myself how clearly Ed visualized this. I answered, clearer than I do. Then I tried to navigate Ed's comet toward pleasure, or at least abstraction, by repeating my father's old joke about violence from on high:

A priest and his friend are playing golf. The friend curses and swears each time he misses the ball. This language upsets the priest who cautions his friend, citing the Bible commandment, but it doesn't do any good. *"Goddam, missed again! Goddam, missed again!"* Then a dark cloud gathers and it discharges a lightning bolt which kills the priest. The friend asks, "Why *him*?" A voice thunders, "Goddam, missed again!"

I agreed it wasn't that funny. We were having coffee and French pastries at the Marie Antoinette Baked Goods concession in Japan Center. Ed chose a gateau: alternating layers of white cake and whipped cream, glazed with dark chocolate. I chose a rum custard. We exchanged tastes. Neither had any flavor more developed than "sweet," they resembled sweet wood. For a time I slid mine around the edge of the plate; it left a wet trail. Its blank cheerfulness demoralized me. Finally I downed it in two big mouthfuls. But I confess I felt happy to see some starch entering Ed's precariously slender body. Ed lives near the edge in so many ways. Long ago I agreed to see him as a porcelain cup held to the lips of "Life itself," with Life about to suffer a loss of muscular tension.

To change the subject, I asked Ed to tell me about his new boyfriend, Tad. I met Tad once and thought he was nice. I could have felt jealous. Consoling myself, I judged it unlikely that anyone would seem more real to Ed than I had seemed, which was not very real. Ed said Tad's parents put him in an orphanage where he lived until he was five. Then he was adopted, but eight years later his new mother decided she didn't want him any longer and she tried to give him back. Tad says that event gave his character its defining cast. But she didn't return him and he went on to become a liberal lawyer. Then San Francisco hired him to reorganize its Police Department, something he was qualified to do. So he sold his house and flew out. He arrived on May 21, 1979, "White Night," the night gays rioted in Civic Center in response to Dan White's nothing sentence for the murder of gay Supervisor Harvey Milk. While Tad was making a phone call at the Elephant Walk, a gay bar on Castro Street, the police charged in. They randomly clubbed people, retaliating on gay turf for the riot on theirs, and the outfit Tad was contracted to reorganize broke three of his ribs. He filed suit for damages, so the city decided not to hire him after all. Meanwhile, the train carrying his furniture and possessions caught fire, taking everything he owned. "Tomorrow," said Ed, "he files for bankruptcy."

Ed ended on almost a note of triumph. "Well," I said, threatened by Tad at last and slightly out of control, "it looks like you've met your match." Ed threw back his head and laughed. He never enjoyed wit unless it was also accurate. As usual, he was doing most of the talking. I supplied nods and supportive lubricating comments, since Ed's life was the place our interests overlapped. Now I felt sullen, withdrawn. Ed replied to my body language. "I know what you mean. Sometimes I lie in bed in a fetal position wishing over and over that I was just one cell, one cell, wishing with all my heart that I was just one cell." I told Ed to shut up. He wavered for a moment. I thought our decade as lovers was dive bombing this tête-à-tête. He had been a battered child. I was losing control. I always assigned a truth too big for me to challenge to his clear, radical unhappiness. Was it just a game—his unhappiness the unreturning ship and myself Penelope at the loom? I didn't trust it anymore. I wanted something else, though I was uncertain what that might be. Hadn't I provided him a safe place and loved him on and off for ten years, giving him as much of the best of myself as he would accept? During that long decade, Ed set a miniature fuchsia branch in a vase, painted spacey canvases of naked heroes rising or falling through pastel distance, charted with his own body an intricate sexuality. I didn't feel betrayed. Instead I willed myself the armor of believing he betrayed himself. My love must be costly, so wasn't its object a pearl beyond price?

When three or four diseases converged, almost killing him, how cool I was, how exemplary; even the night his doctor, avoiding my eyes, told me to get Ed's mother there before morning, leaving it to me to say, "You mean he's going to die?" How toylike, dirty and small the city looked that night. For months I'd start crying out of nowhere, walking Lily or in line at the bank. "At least you didn't die. I should be grateful to you for that," I thought, letting my eyes relax on his face, taking it in with a pleasurable pang, like visiting a childhood home or any place where we've really lived. I apologized: "I don't know what's got into me." I looked up and noticed with distress and amusement that painted on the wall to the right of the counter, circling a stylized Marie Antoinette beaming a cost-effective smile, was the motto *Let them eat cake.*

Our paper plates had been designed to resemble fine china, hand painted. Around the borders the traveling tendrils looped back through the Middle Ages, Dark Ages, Rome and Greece to Sumeria and points east. In the center of mine the queen masquerades as a milkmaid in lyrical caricature of peasants who soon would topple her; in Ed's, the arrogance of a pleasure bower—the lovers united, the slim volume cascades to the grass as it should before that artful embrace. 18th-century lovers on a plate: she smells like ripe strawberries, his scent of frangipani too evident. His right hand points to his heart in the most conventional gesture imaginable. Perfection is easy for them. Like the monks and nuns pictured by my adolescent self, they stake out a little territory along with the teapot, the saucer, and they say, "You see, I do this perfectly." (The implied pair: urgent salty taste of skin and we are really embraced by the low tide odors of seaweed and musk.) This abstract couple bears children and grandchildren—a progeny of adjustments to a violent era: the Victorian in skirts swinging on a moon and singing a microscopic music hall song; and our hero and heroine, murmuring I, I, I, I—they appear infinite in the movie's nearsighted fadeout. The porcelain beau says,

> This crust's exceedingly tender, raspberries,
> Mistress, let me assure you...
> She answers, I am advised...

and the danger from breakage is all or nothing. What do we want? To be absolved of personality, that zero at the center, that Maltese Falcon. Those who embrace personality we make our deities. We envy them and from our poverty they grow rich. Their faces resonate like beehives, or like salmon fishers on a turbulent ocean, the unwilling sweetness rising to the surface like balsa wood.

It's shrewd of these lovers not to trust the body's built-in obsolescence. Their attachment occurs on a high superficial plane where the risk belongs to the viewer. Triumphant, the most delicate Chelsea porcelain, the gold lusters of Dresden, the chaste blue and white of *Porcelaine de Paris.*

The Marie Antoniette Baked Goods concession was beginning to depress me. It wasn't charming at all. It was noisy, it smelled of disinfectant, the chairs weren't comfortable and the food was bad. The acoustics punched holes through our voices and amplified the other sounds. "I was attacked," Ed said. *"What?"* "I was attacked." Did he want to round out our violence motif? Alarmed, I asked if he had been hurt.

He said, "I climbed on a bus at 24th and Mission last Sunday. In the back three teenage boys were shouting about sex—rubbers and how they fucked their girlfriends for five hours. As I sat down they switched to antigay remarks. That went on. When another gay man boarded the bus they became louder and more vicious. My stop came up—I was concerned about the other gay man. I wanted him to get off with me or else I would stay on until his stop. Instead, I stood helpless by the back door while they stepped up their insults. I turned and looked at the lead guy, we exchanged stares. I got off the bus; as it pulled away we were still staring and I said *Fuck You.* He couldn't have heard me but I knew he would understand. He pulled the cord, the bus stopped and they got out and started following me. I speeded up. Every time I looked back at them I wanted to say I was sorry—I wanted to hug them and say, please don't let it be like this. I thought if I start running they'll start running, but they were catching up. I started running with ease. I kept thinking, this is so easy, everything in slow motion. When I turned around to look, the lead pulled out a nine inch ice pick and the others had six inch blades. They started running hard at me. I ran with all my force, thinking that if Kito's front door is locked I'm dead. I thought that was it. They caught up with me and began surrounding me just as I burst into Kito's Bar. I threw my body at the door. I flew in—knocked two women to the floor. A huge woman bouncer grabbed me and started shaking me and then I really got frightened. Once in, I knew I could be as afraid as I wanted. I'm talking and gasping, what just happened, I got weak in the knees and started to collapse. Some women grabbed me and sat me in a chair and bought me a beer, while the bouncer and two women chased the teenagers away."

Ed and I were both on the verge of tears. We felt everything: nervous, helpless, scared, angry. I was angry at Ed for jeopardizing what I had taken such good care of, his life. I was angry at the world and tired of being a person. The tiredness felt like an itch I couldn't reach. We were as baffled as our times; violence from the skies, the police, the streets—legions invade us in babysteps, readjusting chemical responses, altering vision, so that a specter steps out of a void, shoots, blows smoke from the barrel, steps back. How many ways can we duck when we carry the explosion inside? Still, Ed's story was clear. He boarded a bus and someone tried to kill him.

We halfheartedly discussed a self-protection class on the use of Mace offered by CUAV, a gay community group. As we gathered ourselves to leave, Ed said, "You're flying to LA?"

"Yes, tomorrow." "I probably shouldn't say this, but I've been having premonitions, and I had one about your plane. I think it's going to crash." "If it does," I said, "I want you to know I forgive you almost everything." I was angry at him, and didn't stop being angry until the wheels of my return flight touched the runway.

TWO STORIES ABOUT VIOLENCE:

Outside a bar two men grab me, push me into an alley, whisper intimately, *Faggot*. A cold spot on the back of my head and then bang!—one more dead queer. That happened, but not to me.

I was at the grocery store picking up a few things. I checked out and headed home, thinking of Sarah Vaughan singing "I've Got the World on a String," the song filled with a joy that holds enough irony for me to trust it. A small dinner ahead, discrete flavors, fresh peppercorns in the rice for instance, anise root in the salad. A new friend, maybe. I'll stop for flowers. Ranunculus, utterly focused. I wear a smile—everyone smiles at me if I carry flowers or a white bakery box tied with a string. Kathleen: flower— ranunculus, flavor—lemon. Ed: freesia, raspberry. Denise: tulip, chocolate (both Dutch). Tommy: ranunculus, vanilla. It's a balmy Sunday evening; San Francisco looks rested and blousy and suddenly I am surrounded by fourteen teenage boys shouting, "We're gonna get you, fag!" And that's exactly what they do, with their fists, their feet, several bottles and some pieces of scrap metal. Their blows hurt less and less.

My glasses and packages are scattered. Colors begin to bleach out. I think—detached—surely I'm strapped to a fiery wheel: a dislocated hip, a bruised liver, kidney damage, lung damage, bruises and lacerations. A young man calls the police but when they arrive they throw my ID in the garbage where it vanishes like a white stone dropped in milk. As they take me away, I notice a splotch of my blood on the ground. To leave it pierces me with sentimental regret. That happened, but not to me.

Before I get to Ed and the orchid farm, I'd like to tell you about the long drives my family used to take in our red Plymouth station wagon. We drove to visit the zoo in San Diego, or Solvang to eat pea soup and bread baked with onion and cheese that my father liked, or Santa Barbara to see the mission and the botanical garden, or Big Bear to catch trout, or Yosemite, or Denver or the East. We would squabble for a while and then settle into the shared experience of propulsion, working out song arrangements, descants and counterpoints, making up games to assist the mileage. One game we played was "Reincarnation," that is, we would say what we wanted to come back as. My mother would choose something nice: a peony, generous flower, or a bird from 19th-century poetry, a hummingbird. My father characteristically turned the game into a joke. He chose to return as Prince, Mr. Schneck's toy French poodle who resided in Beverly Hills. Prince was my dad's symbol for life on Easy Street. My characteristic choice would be the rose window at Chartres.

"The rose window at Chartres?" exclaimed Ed. "They should have stopped the car and spanked you!"

I laughed. Of course Ed was right. He meant I tried to bully my family with knowledge. And you can bet the game and my choice weren't religious. We believed in God to the exact degree that we could attend temple services without being two-faced hypocrites. A hummingbird, a French poodle, a rose window — could these be the building blocks of my personality?

Or it was religious. Later, in high school, I started reading 14th- and 15th-century Christian devotional literature, and I alarmed my family with the news that I wanted to join a monastery. Judaism didn't provide a place to hide away. "You're afraid of life," my mother said mildly. "That's right," I answered. I was surprised she mentioned it. Wasn't she? — my father? — everyone else? Beyond that, a certain word was growing in me, a word too charged for the newspapers, for books, TV, even for my father's jokes. When I located *Homosexual* under *H* in the index of library psychology books, the sight of it jarred me, my stomach clenched — blushing, I averted my eyes. It went way beyond fuck, shit or piss; in its clinical remoteness it went beyond nigger, dago, spick, kike; it would grow and become large as I was, equaling me. If the word was so despised, what would become of me once I had given it corporeal form?

Anyway, I didn't see the derring in the stories I read about those 15th-century lives: "Thus I dured till day, and by then my body was dead from the middle downwards, as to my feeling. After this my sight began to fail, and it was all dark about me in the chamber, as if it had been night, save in the Image of the Cross, whereon I beheld a common light; and I wist not how. All that was away from the Cross was of horror to me, as if it had been greatly occupied by fiends. After this the upper part of my body began to die, so far forth that scarcely I had any feeling—with shortness of breath. And then I weened in sooth to have passed." Dame Julian of Norwich was not looking for a safe option.

You would be surprised at the number of gay men who start life intending to take holy orders—it's a ready-made community, a chance to exercise our famous altruism, and *safety*. "Of course you want safety," says Freud, stroking his celestial beard. "It's because homosexuals are paranoid. They imagine everyone is against them." He never mentions that this may be a realistic point of view. When God visits the paranoid Dr. Schreber, the Father of Creation yells, "Scoundrel!" Voices assure Dr. Schreber that his proposed transformation into a woman is an abomination. The world's contempt crushes him, so he gathers his shattered gestures and rewrites them, elevating his degradation by staging it as cosmic drama. But isn't it Freud's disease too? Frankly, Freud's bemused objectivity repels me, it's a violence that colludes with the disease; we wait in vain for him to say that being a woman is not contemptible.

As an alternate answer to hummingbird and peony, my mother sometimes took an opposite tack. She would choose a Clydesdale, a workhorse, wryly alluding to her daily mountain of drudgery and the minimal thanks she garnered. My father would chime in and say about the person he loves most in the world and who remains his polestar, "When she gets to heaven they'll give her a bale of hay and call her a horse's ass." Groan. I draw your attention to these answers, and Freud, and my father because this is a story about violence, so I must talk about the language of the fathers.

When my parents threw a party the men would eventually group in the upholstered living room, drinking

Scotch and sodas, discussing politics and trading jokes under the family portraits. Every one of these Democrats held a different point of view and a consensus was not necessary or even desirable.

"You say integration, but in 1937 there was this colored fellow who worked in my mattress factory on Buckeye Road who...." It was not all as bad as that. The rivalry was gentle and the point was for everyone to talk, to keep the talk going in an endless river that didn't need to arrive at any ocean.

Morrie Rolf lounges expansively, savoring the expensive bitterness of his cigar, then carries it aloft with surprising delicacy, thumb and forefinger. On the flocked wallpaper, Morrie's shadow aims a lightning bolt whose girth and angle suggest an upwardly mobile target. Morrie says, "How do you figure that the Egyptians got ten plagues in Egypt, but fifty plagues at sea? The Bible says, 'And the magicians said to Pharaoh: It is the *finger* of God!'" Here Morrie holds up an ironic finger. A diamond on a heavy gold band sparkles to itself. "And when they reached the Red Sea? 'And Israel saw the *great hand* which the Lord laid upon the Egyptians.'" Morrie holds up five fingers; the sleeve of his navy blue blazer, chosen by Doreen, slips down over a silk shirt, also chosen by Doreen, on which every African sunset color splashes together, attesting to her love for the world. "How many plagues by one finger? *Ten!* So it only makes sense that they sustained *ten* plagues in Egypt and *fifty* plagues at sea." His cigar underlines the numbers.

But Bill Gross says temperately, "How do we know that each of Morrie's plagues was really four plagues? 'He sent them the kindling of his wrath, anger, and gloom, and trouble, a legation of evil angels.' Anger—one; gloom—two;

trouble—three; a legation of angels—four. So they received forty plagues in Egypt and two hundred plagues at sea." His eyes are warm, his hands remain folded over the Perry Como sweater Helen chose for him, he easily yields the floor.

Mr. Pochras leaps in with his big "gimme" voice. "I'll show you that each plague which the Holy One (blessed is He) brought on the Egyptians consisted of five plagues." He sits forward, broadly gesticulates. "He sent them the kindling of his wrath? *Bubeleh* forgot to count the kindling of his wrath!" He puts his hand on Bill's knee, a caress. "I figure it this way: Wrath—*one!* Anger—*two!* Gloom—*three!* Trouble—*four!* Evil angels—*five!* So they received fifty plagues in Egypt and two hundred fifty plagues at sea." He sits back grinning, intensely pleased with himself, all chest, neck and head.

Well, that's a fine point for sure, there's God's wrath and there's God's anger. I wonder which one Ed sees when he closes his eyes. But their verbal exercise was just that; like dogs playing they went through the motions of aggression, chase and lunge for the jugular, preparing their real fight to subdue the world, because most of these men used words to earn a living, whether as teachers, salesmen or lawyers. So the Old Testament arms deployed by my heroic forefathers became a verbal tournament staged by my less heroic but more recognizable uncles in the 2nd century—Rabbi Josei the Galilean, Rabbi Eliezer and Rabbi Akiba. I've more or less lifted this conversation from the Passover *Haggadah,* cut from the same cloth as my seniors' debates. Their subtlety gives heavenly violence a hallucinatory abstraction. Possibly the story of Moses touched those 2nd century rabbis more than the Korean war moved their remote grandsons, but foregrounded for both is the thrill of verbal manipulation. They withdrew the emotion from the content and applied themselves to form. Contempt is woven into the very texture of this language. First emotion is withdrawn, then it is assigned to women and gays, and then we are needed because without us life would be barren. But we embody what has been dismissed, so why not roll a fag? At the same time, form allows art, it allows distance. I revamped Ed's daydream of an Oakland planetary upheaval into a joke *(Goddam, missed again!)* to be assessed on aesthetic grounds. Where did I fail? I left out history: people as they shape events, events as they shape people.

I thought all these men were windbags. The sweetness of their discourse was lost on me. They were full of hot air and maybe they knew and enjoyed it. My father would joke, "Your mother makes the small decisions, like where we live and where I work. She leaves the big ones, like Southeast Asia, to me." I didn't grasp that some of these friendships were a lifetime old; that these men had set each other up in business, worked side by side, suffered deaths, WPA projects, applauded each other's babies, shared apartments, relatives and innumerable holidays; and that their conversations were studded with subterranean "I love you's."

My father begins without a prologue. "There was a golfer, he *loved* golf. He was avid for it." He pauses, everyone's convinced. "Then one day the Devil comes up to him on the fairway. He says, 'Look, how would you like to improve your game?' " My father looks down, studying the situation, then looks up, intrigued. All time is at my father's disposal, balanced against the exigencies of the plot. "Wellll—what do I have to pay you?" The Devil answers, his hand gesturing to my father's friends, "Your sex life isn't going to be so good." They laugh a little anxiously. He has mastered the room and now he leisurely collects the love (in the form of attention) which he has generated. The golfer decides to agree, and they meet a year later. The Devil says, "Tell me, how was your game?" "Terrific! My drives are great, putting great, I'm so and so many points below par—everything's great!" (Pause.) "How about your sex life?" "Great, just great." (A high wire pause.) *Really?* Tell me about it. How often did you do it?" "Three times this year!" The Devil laughs, my father's face is resonant, he hushes his voice, says intimately, "Say, just three times?" Already his friends are laughing; soon their faces will be contorted as in extreme grief and that release will exclude my father. His house of cards will go up in that blast. He concludes almost regretfully, "Sure, three times. Not bad for a small town priest."

The stand-up joke: a self-contained unit of humor that does not require a clown, a Gracie Allen, a Fanny Brice. Architecture expresses the stand-up joke as a skyscraper, they share the same historical period. Maybe a century ago my dad, with his art and his bottomless memory, would have been the town storyteller, the good counselor. The one about the mermaid and the man with a small head, the one about the oversexed rooster, the one about three doctors and a tailor, the one about the anti-Semitic parrot, the rabbi and the minister and the priest, the black man and his disease (what looks bad but feels good?), the man who finds a gorilla on his roof, the funeral of the wife and the mother-in-law, the Italian miner, the moose and the $10 bar drink, the black preacher ("Who *says* the organ player is a motherfucker?"), the traveling salesman, the traveling salesman, the traveling salesman, the traveling salesman, the traveling salesman. I want to name and pass over their burden of sexual prowess and anxiety, sexism and bigotry, hostility and homoeroticism, burbling along together.

If these men snarled, "We think women are despicable," history would have entered drawing battle lines, but their "universal" contempt was the flip side of Schreber's "universal" paranoia. The language of objectivity denies the snarl, and to the degree we possess this language, we are possessed by it. As for the content, the passion for form provided an escape clause: it was only a joke, a discussion, a theoretical workout. That their world became gradually less real was no help. Most had moved away from extended families, houses on streets where neighbors were friends and relatives right up the block. They moved to suburban tracts and bedroom communities, each family isolated, "a good place to raise children"; far away from history, from the hard victories and defeats, the flux of events.

I think of their generation as America's middle children. Their immigrant parents got the best and the worst; striding two centuries and two cultures in the salad days of capitalism, their lives become legends. The plot was simple whether fulfilled or not: to go from poverty to security. Their dilated Central European eyes remain in my family album on the top shelf of a linen closet. As for my parents' generation, their vices and virtues are too often on a smaller scale, the potential not fully expressed, their lives measured against the bric-a-brac of their parents' desires, the upholstered tokens of security which eventually became confused with security itself. And my generation, aren't we the babies? — overprotected adolescence lasting until thirty while we make claims on our parents' promise that we would be happy and free, claims which enlarged themselves into the counterculture movements of the sixties. What generation has been so attended to that a new word—teenager—was coined to prolong our childhood?

The jokes these men told were mostly about sex, and now I remember that sex was the nominal reason the men and women separated. The men cheerfully complained that their wives couldn't tell a joke and they were right. That static form wasn't for women, perhaps because mutual support, never mentioned in the living room, was the theme in the kitchen. The women gathered around the table, getting high on cake and coffee. That's where I stayed. To put it mildly, their talk made more sense to me. This distinction echoed the one at school. The boys chased balls, different kinds according to the season, back and forth across the school yard. How much nicer, wittier really, to hang by my knees from the jungle gym in a row with the girls, discussing who's nice, who's terrible and why, while our faces reddened from our upside down blood. The women's talk was sharper, less inhibited. The wit was based on mimicry, on accurate portrayals of daily events, personal stories. Lois Cogan imitated ample Eileen Farrell being schlepped back and forth across the stage by tottering flamenco dancers while reluctantly singing the Habanera on *Ed Sullivan.* She became at once Farrell, the dancers and the appalled audience. Everyone was giddy from laughter. Doreen would describe some treasured act of derring-do by heroines she knew personally, like Flossie Klein smoking a cigar in front of the rabbi. There was validation of labor and endless trading of emotions and praise. (After some clever problem-solving by my mother—say, using the vacuum cleaner to eliminate a row of ants or pick flies out of the air—Doreen Rolf turns to me: "Bobby, your mother's a genius!" and gives her a big kiss.)

The secrets of food, dramatic fire sales, children's dilemmas and achievements, the pressing details of the maintenance of life: these made sense to me. Still, what was missing from each group the other could have provided. The women could have linked their world to the larger one, saying, "After World War Two the government brainwashed us into giving up our jobs and becoming homemakers." The men could have said, "Ronnie is flunking third grade—because all he thinks about is the atom bomb."

I admired these women who were housewives as later—briefly—I admired people who took monastic vows. I apprenticed myself to their language and action, and I am bound to say that I can clean a house, I know what solvent to use for what dirt, that cornstarch is best for windows, my apple pie is famous, for love my bread levitates off the pan, and my pot roast—the sovereign of meats—tasting and tasting—and I can iron a pleated skirt. Later I learned muscley skills: to hang a door, restring a window. I learned how to fashion wood. I lean into the work like the man in the WPA murals. Cutting is dangerous and hurts. Sanding is praise. Bringing up the grain is praise; against that buttery surface the grain demonstrates, twisting and boiling up from below. A piece of cedar looks like Japanese art or a western sunset; English oak—tightgrained, Keatsean; American oak monitors sunlight into the comfortable and uncomfortable 19th century. I learned the language of shim shingles, cant strips, flashing, 16 penny sinkers, joists and studs, stucco molding, baseboard and crown molding, drains and vents, caulking, building adhesive, cripple studs, drive screws and z-bar. And I learned to frame my anger and aggression, squaring off my argument into objective truths, the rock of ages, unassailable. I always wanted to be a great husband and wife, and a child too, who eats up the gingerbread house.

See this as a gay man's strategy to house mother and father safely inside himself. But these interior figures suffer like their counterparts until the question, "Will I ever be normal?" yields before future developments, challenging and canceling the question itself. What will the new question be? A tableau: Father, mother, sister and brother picnic by a lake dappled with trout. The sun slants to make them small and highly three-dimensional. Junior skips pebbles across the water, mastering the lake. Sister sits politely on a rock, internalizing the scratches on her new Mary Janes. Hormones course through them, pushing out breasts, fiercely enlarging genitals, changing hair patterns—legs, armpits, groin and face; manicuring, cinching waists, giving her an ass, him shoulders and calves, touching everywhere, percolating. She follows her brother's stone saying, "My body, her body, his body, your body."

ONE STORY ABOUT VIOLENCE:

Larry and I were getting into my car last Monday night after visiting a bar to share a beer and some talk. We were both depressed, lonely, making the best of things but weighed down by a sense of failure. I had been sharp and clear—people like that—but now unhappiness suggested a dozen directions. I could have said anything, made a joke, cried. Suddenly five or six men in their early twenties surrounded my car. We locked the doors but one said, "Open this door, faggot." I looked up the barrel of his gun. I was nauseated, taking in too much information: a scar on his finger, a frayed sleeve, a bent stop sign at the comer; the night lifted and heaved toward black and red, twisting licorice colors. "So this is the time and the place." I almost couldn't negotiate the locked door. Fortunately they didn't use the gun. One of them caught my arms, the others punched at my stomach and face. I caught a tilted view of Larry. He had curled against a fender, silent while they kicked him in the back. In his black ski jacket he looked like a broken umbrella. I pictured his rows of books. I began calling them names but without conviction—my words sounded lame and foreign even to myself. A wave of nausea—nothing—then a clammy lift into consciousness. They had taken our wallets.

That happened, but not to us. I don't want this for anyone. You don't want this for anyone. I say *I* and *you* because pain should have its unmistakable identity.

About a month after our coffee and pastry episode, I drove Ed to the Rod McLellan Orchid Farm in South San Francisco. The trip came under the rubric of a favor, but I hadn't been there in four years and really I just wanted the excuse to go. On the way down I told him a dream in which I saw two new varieties of grasshopper. One had wings like luminous scarves, the other's wings were Boston fern fronds. Then I felt a sensual tingling on my scalp; I had grown thick moss there, giant maidenhair and bracken ferns and bromeliads. I looked a little like Carmen Miranda. Ed replied that one day Dean, a fellow waiter, bragged to the staff that he earned $1000 a performance singing French folk songs at parties; then he pulled Ed aside and whispered, "I do Piaf in high drag!"

Ed intended to learn about dividing and repotting orchids and when we arrived a very nice woman showed us how. She seemed permanently amused; I wondered if that's characteristic of orchid growers. I notice at the Farmers' Market that the fruit people are always happier than the vegetable people. Maybe the smell of orchids tickled her. I remember whole neighborhoods that smelled like cabbage, like sauerkraut, and that's the way the residents behaved, carried themselves.

Orchid dividing was complicated and beautiful. Her intelligent fingers constantly caressed the plant while they judged the proximity of the pods, the direction of the roots—trimming them and clearing out old bark, tenderly combing them like hair, snipping ones that were old and decayed. The building held the special greenhouse light that could only be brighter if direct, only moister in a downpour, charged with the patience and expectancy of new growth; the quietly jubilant air chock full of light and absolutely still, heavy and soft, so that Ed and I whispered to each other.

Ed had arrived with one orchid, now he had two. We left them with the woman and strolled around the miles of greenhouse looking at the flowers. The gentility of the place would have bothered me—rich people boarded plants there between blooms—but Ed's presence gave the outing a pleasantly urgent feeling. His relation to the plants was direct. He grew up in the lush rain forests of Hawaii; his Japanese mother lived with her Buddhist parents in a guava grove on Hilo where she met his father, a military man of German Jewish descent. Ed's response to the beauty of plants was unmediated and they gave him their best. Under his auspices even the modest philodendron bloomed, producing a big white penis wrapped in a waxy red bandanna. I enjoyed this beauty by proxy, having no trusted feel for it myself. A few years before, with the idea that plants should pull their own weight, I built four wooden planters on the back porch and filled them with dirt and romaine lettuce seeds. They grew, but one day I was alarmed to see that the plants had turned larval white. When I touched a leaf, the white detached itself and flew into my face and hair like a delirium. Whitefly. Nauseated, I fled and I didn't return until the bugs finished the lettuce and died for lack of food. Then I took one of the planters and turned it into a window box for the kitchen. I planted a row of tulips in it. They grew up horribly deformed—a comment—then withdrew into the dirt. Then weeds took over the box. They were like mutts, hearty and confident. All I asked for was a little greenery that looked as though it enjoyed life, so I let them grow.

Certainly I thought a poet should know the language of flowers but Ed's knowledge was so complete I felt knowing him was enough. We wandered through the square miles, a tropical park, chatting and browsing, gloved by the nutritious air. Finally we paused in front of a display of the rarest orchids. They were not for sale. We pointed out the beauties to each other. Ed is an artist; I relied on the accuracy of his eye, his ability to give a name to spatial relationships and colors. The orchids corresponded one to one with Ed in his various incarnations. The *paphiopedilum sukhakulli,* "The Giant," black and white wings, tough little face and pugnacious jaw, was Ed in black leather jacket and scraggly face hair, punky, touching to the degree that the outfit misrepresented his softness and high elegance. The effect was of a Shakespearean heroine who dressed as a man. The cattleya, "Lucilla," with its obviousness, its big outrageous purples, the color shimmering like a cave lake, was Ed when he dyed his hair bullet blue. In the sunlight it cast a technicolor halo, making him tactilely remote and visually huge. The oncidium, fireworks of tiny flowers, was Ed when I first met him waiting at a bus stop. One orchid expert writes, "Picture a troupe of dancers at some country fair, their swirling costumes awash with warm yellow, rose, soft brown and white." In those days Ed wore flower child robes and his hair fell halfway down his back—a chrysanthemum on a long swaying stem. Flashes of our sexual life together: being fucked luxuriously, all systems go, and then he lightly grazes my nipple which makes me come; scooping up his sperm to use as a lubricant; admiring his El Greco torso—fingering a nipple, I say, "I always wanted to have a chest like that." "Good," he answers, "now you've got one." And then afterward Lily lumbers onto the bed, settles down between us, crosses her paws and takes up the heavy breathing where we left off.

Ed asked after Jeff and Sally, mutual friends, which reminded me of a Berkeley party I wanted to describe. Driving there, Bruce, Denise and I supposed that this particular world was small; we wondered who we would see. It was a Greek Easter outdoor banquet staged by a Greek Stalinist professor and his Lebanese wife, who was multilingual and baked pastry for Chez Panisse. They were friends of Martin, a formidable art historian and our ticket to this feast. The food was amazing. A whole lamb turned on a spit, its roasted organs ceremoniously eaten in an observance that dated, said our host at some length, to the very dawn of man. There were small complex almond tortes, fried cheese pies, walnut rolls, sweet Easter breads, stuffed grape leaves, filo dough pastries filled with lamb and feta cheese, and retsina and ouzo to drink. A savory spiced meat was passed around. Someone called it pastrami. I said no. Someone else said pastrami is smoked camel meat. "Not unless it's a kosher camel," I replied. Martin suggested that first you capture a bear, then torture it until it admits it's a camel, then smoke it.

The wood fire bristled, urgent, while these Berkeley citizens released their slower heat. They were well-behaved: a long bench bisected the yard and most of them sat on it, facing the same direction like passengers in a train station. Above, muscular young Berkeley men and women ascended and descended the sheer face of Cragmont Rock, an Indian holy place and public park. I wondered how they felt about blaring Greek music and lamb smoke; water off a duck's back, I decided. I wondered what could unify these cultural shards, these random quotations—alcohol? I poured a stiff glass of ouzo and became tipsy and started flirting with Martin, who flirted back, and who also flirted with Denise, who was doing some flirting of her own. Liz, Martin's wife, a scholar in her own right, also flirted. I felt so frisky, I wondered why I didn't drink more often. Something crouching in me stood up straight and had fun. Our "novelty acts" vanished, taking aggression with them. I assumed the world was gearing up to embrace itself, so the nuances and ramifications of everything were lost on me, but Bruce explained them later. Meanwhile, the guests beamed and radiated, accepting breath as though a high wind roared against our faces. Or we rushed through quiet air—I sucked it through my teeth—each cell was a swing my heart pushed higher and higher—it was ravishing until it was nauseating. Smiling shyly I excused myself, skirted through the expensive house on xylophone tiptoes and vomited gently in the bathroom.

Ed shifted, he was losing interest. Moreover, through a trick of light his dark irises gathered the brightness into disconcerting pinpoints. Taking his elbow, I led him a few steps to the right but the pinpoints remained, so I sped up to the important part of the story.

Anyway, who should step out of the back door and into the sunlight but Jeff and Sally—surprise and embraces all around. They were arguing. Not arguing, Jeff said, but having a debate. Not having a debate, I told Ed, but arguing. It was about an exalted French philosopher who used "phallus" to describe any thrust of power—especially language manipulation. Sally revolted against such a term and I—despite the summer-into-fall decline my drunkenness had taken—leapt into the fray. "What would you say if instead of your cock he used Sally's cunt to designate power?" Jeff blanched. "Phallus! Phallus! He didn't mean cock." Jeff had wanted a friendly debate, a sign of friendship, an abstract wrestling match concluded by a handshake, a good winner, a good loser. Clearly that could not occur if our cocks were the same as Jeff's phallus, a piece of psychic anatomy to which Sally could aspire on learning how to murder with language. And after all, the rabbis were not vexed by the number of plagues, they just wanted to talk about them. What if an Egyptian entered their debate saying, "These frogs and boils and locusts *happened* to me!" He would have spoiled everything. That's what I was doing.

My friendship with Jeff is a decade old. I call him when I have news; if I am in trouble, I ask him to help me. Then why, in the space of a phrase, do we become enemies? Perhaps the language itself generates aggression. Still, none of us was simple enough to think this contest was only about the phallus. The phallus had become a small country on which we mounted our big war.

As Sally and I surrounded Jeff, he became more subtle. Jeff was right to be worried; once you fall off the observation platform it's hard to climb back on. I said I didn't trust objectivity divorced from stated goals, emotions. The emotion will always creep back in the form of contempt. I piously cited proofs, authorities. That was an argument Jeff couldn't refute so he didn't, he agreed and then went right on—"If you *could* speak that way—" Sally interrupted him. "Why not begin with how you feel, what this language does to you?" Jeff cast her a withering look. "This is a discourse in the world—you have to understand it. You never get beyond your feelings." He seemed to think that life was merely a garden yielding food for thought.

"I see your point of view," I countered. "You want to roam down the highways and byways of a given structure. Do you see our point of view?" He did not. He accused Sally and me of "Solidarity," which he dismissed as a buzz word. Sally said, "I thank my lucky stars that I have some tools to fight your contempt with." Jeff lapsed into a dispirited silence, an equal mix of sadness and disdain. That finished our debate; we did not part genially and I didn't know what was gained.

The next day I found a note from Sally in my mailbox. She began: "Uncomfortable, yes; unfair, perhaps. I am thinking a lot this morning about change and how it happens, how it grows." I felt anxious. I thought, "Not enough, not in time." Still, I could see she was right. Sally went on to remind me that a few years ago when faced with a contest we took a walk. We took walks when the talk seemed hopelessly dominated or when we were being quietly dismissed. At the end of the letter she said to me and I said to Ed, "We became stronger, we changed for the better."

Ed caught my joy. I wanted him to understand and he showed me he did—he gave story for story.

He told me that he'd taken the Mace course that CUAV sponsored. CUAV stands for Community United Against Violence. "One night," he said, "I heard a man and woman yelling at each other across the street. The woman was screaming and then I heard thuds that rattled my dishes. I ran to the window and looked out. The man had grasped the woman by her breasts and he pounded her back into the sidewalk. I threw on some shoes, pants and a jacket, grabbed my Mace and ran to about ten feet away from the man. That's the distance Mace shoots. By then the woman had got up. She was pleading with him but he punched her in the chest and she fell backward. I had passed a group of five people; they were milling and watching but I wouldn't let myself believe they were just standing there. I aimed the Mace. I stood like my dad." Ed used to mime his father's macho stance, a parody: He affected a butch scowl, a ferocious pout. He thrust his hips forward, tensed his eyes and spread his legs so that, as Ed would explain to me, his balls could hang free. "I aimed the Mace at his heart and yelled, 'Stop. This is Mace. I've been trained by the police. Let go of her.' I felt terrified but very sure of myself. He stood up—that's when I saw he was enormous. I'm still sorry I didn't Mace him but I was afraid of hitting her. I knew I was doing right, I was secure in that thought. I knew if I gave him second degree burns or even blinded him it was OK. He had something in his hand; I was afraid it was a gun, so I situated myself behind a parking meter. Then I took two big steps forward and screamed again. He just dropped her and took a step back. I took a step forward, still aiming, my arm stretched out. I yelled, 'Go!' We repeated that whole sequence: I stepped forward, yelled, 'Go,' he retreated a step. I almost wasn't believing what was happening—it seemed out of control and unreal. Finally he turned and walked into the night. Then I went to the woman and helped her up. She was panic-stricken—her glasses smashed, her purse, coat and shoes scattered. I urged her to come with me and call the police but she refused. One of the spectators, a woman, came up and started holding her. She told me that she'd take care of her, take her to the bar, clean her up and call the police."

"Why Ed, you're a hero!" I embraced him. I was really impressed. Ed went on to say that CUAV asked him to testify at antigay violence hearings; he accepted despite his terror at the prospect. In this way he would challenge a giant silence that has become so routine we hardly notice it. It expresses itself when we hear—as we do—that another gay man killed himself. We plunge and surface with it. I felt a predictable welling up of resistance; I'd be obliged to say goodbye to a part of Ed I relied on as a touchstone. But this violence was not from "on high" and Ed put his anger where it belonged—he would have added a faceful of Mace. I took this fighting back to be a sign of structural change in his life—all our lives—and I felt deeply grateful to him. And he gave me the happy ending I wanted for this story: provisional, I know, as any ending that's not a death; hard won, in that we depend on "change" for our happy endings, but the will to change must be grounded in the world as it is, difficult, alien, with a language that slips away. Embarrassment and awkwardness—Ed, who's graceful as a cat, marched woodenly forward yelling "Go!" And I regret my eager unfairness to Jeff— I wanted to bully him. If he had let down his defenses, would I have let down mine? Still, you can't start in the middle. I take my father's aggression, his perhaps wrongheaded confidence that language can generate love, and my mother's steady concentration on social relations and the maintenance of life, adding to this formula our gathering belief in change.

I wanted to relish this minute between Ed and me but we were suddenly surrounded by a group of suburban orchid enthusiasts and a noisy dog. "Maybe he's got fleas?" a woman ventured. Not wanting to offend, she backtracked to "What's his name?" "Ralph"—much chuckling. Ralph was a nondescript terrier mix. The first woman said, "Angela! I thought I saw you but I said no, but here you are. People don't change. I don't care what they say. I look in the mirror and I don't see a difference." Angela replied, "There's nothing wrong with Ralph as far as biting somebody or anything like that. My other bared his teeth and wouldn't stop when I hit him in the snout. I like friendly ones." "For pets," the first woman added. "You should have his tail bobbed. You want to go home with me? My goodness! You want to play!" "He wants to see *everything*," said Angela's husband. Ralph broke for the door. Stay. Stay. Stay. Stay. "See how nice he stays?" "What's his name?—Ralph?" Laughter. "We got him from the pound and that was his name. He was already named Ralph." Laughter. "He minds. That's a good boy. That's a good boy. You sit."

Poor Ralph, the world remained the world. It was time to leave. Ed and I walked back to the car, each carrying half of Ed's divided orchid. We decided to go to Andy's, a cafe on 17th off Castro, where they make the best French fries. As we were enjoying that classic American combination of ketchup, salt and grease, Ed said he wanted me to have one of the orchids. It was an oncidium—"Picture dancers at some country fair." I pictured them.